High School High

A PORT CITY HIGH NOVEL

SHANNON
FREEMAN

SADDLEBACK
PUBLISHING

High School High

Taken

Deported

The Public Eye

www.sdlback.com

ISBN-13: 978-1-62250-037-6
ISBN-10: 1-62250-037-7
eBook: 978-1-61247-680-3

Printed in Guangzhou, China
NOR/0713/CA21301345

17 16 15 14 13   2 3 4 5 6

ACKNOWLEDGMENTS

First I have to thank the wonderful people who inspire my characters: my family, friends, and students alike. Your lives and stories have kept me entertained for years, and I am humbled for our lives to reach out and touch others. Though no character can truly be one of you, there is a small piece of each of you in all of them.

There are so many people who made this manuscript into the work of art that it is today. Those who were the first eyes of my vision for Port City High, thank you for spending time critiquing, correcting, and supporting my work.

Thanks to my husband, Derrick, for helping me every step of the way. Thank you to my mother, Carolyn, for being one of the first to read my story and loving it from the onset. Also, thank you to Nicole McCafni for being my second eyes and helping make this possible.

A special thanks to Saddleback for seeing the potential of a new author, thirsty to tell a story.

—Shannon Freeman

DEDICATION

To my wonderful husband and beautiful children ... you inspire me to achieve greatness.

Prologue

"Here we are, standing on the threshold of forever," Shane said to her friends as she gazed at the building where they would spend the next four years of their lives.

"Gosh, Shane, you are so dramatic," responded Marisa.

"But that's what you love about me, Mari." Shane smiled.

Marisa, Brandi, and Shane never took their eyes off the ominous building in front of them, Port City High. It was the only high school in the small Texas town of Port City, a place that would not appear on the map if the oil refineries had not made it their home. It was the first day of school for the three best friends, and they just stood there, soaking in the moment. "Well, ladies, this is it," Brandi announced. The girls couldn't hide their excitement, but they were also pretty nervous. They were on a high school high and loving it.

"Port City High won't know what hit 'em," Shane said while twirling her pencil. The girls were on top of the world. They had met earlier at Marisa's house to get ready for their big day. They lived blocks apart in a quiet neighborhood, where middle class families enjoyed a simple life. The homes were large and had once belonged to the wealthiest residents of Port City, who had moved on to larger cities when the economy slowed. The former estates made perfect homes for growing families.

Traditionally, the girls would meet up to put the finishing touches on their school uniforms. Their school colors this year were sky blue, silver, and white, so the girls each chose a color the night before and rocked it with their khakis.

Marisa Maldonado wore a white top to compliment her beautiful brown skin. Her hair was dark and curly, but she straightened it when the humid Texas weather permitted. Over the summer Marisa had grown very tall, which was perfect for her. She knew many girls who hated being tall; but she wanted to be a model one day, so the taller, the better.

Shane Foster wore a sky blue uniform shirt that fit her just snug enough to show how flawlessly she was shaped. She loved light colors. Her skin was only a few shades darker than Marisa's, even though Marisa was Hispanic and she was mixed. Shane had the kind of beauty that allowed her to wear barely any makeup. When she went places, people seemed drawn to her. They would ask, "Do you know how beautiful you are?" She knew that others found her extremely attractive. She never allowed herself to get a big head, though, which only made her more appealing.

Brandi Haywood was African American and had the curves to prove it. Many people said that she was the prettiest chocolate girl at school. Brandi chose to wear silver to contrast with her dark skin, making it bling like platinum. Brandi's style and walk were her greatest assets. Her head was always held high, and she looked confident in any situation.

The girls each added their own swag to stand out in the masses. In middle school other girls would try to compete with them but just wound up hating instead. Now they had new land to conquer: high school.

"I guess we should find out where we are supposed to be," announced Brandi as the three of them strolled to the door.

When they entered, they were greeted by Mrs. Monroe. "O-M-G! Mrs. Monroe, what are you doing here?" asked Shane. Mrs. Monroe was the girls' favorite English teacher in middle school.

"The district moved me to Port City High. I'm the new speech and journalism teacher. So you have to put up with me for four more years. The ninth graders are meeting in the cafeteria, so follow the green line down the hall. You can't miss it. And, ladies?"

"Yes, Mrs. Monroe?"

"Have a great time at your new school."

"Thank you, Mrs. Monroe," the girls responded.

They followed the green line. When they walked in the cafeteria, it was already packed with ninth graders. "This should be interesting," Shane said.

"Let's just find a seat," Brandi remarked. The girls located three seats and quickly sat down.

As soon as they were seated, the principal, Mrs. Montgomery, began to address their class. She gave them directions for the day and dismissed them to their homerooms, where they would receive class schedules. The three friends each had a different homeroom. They looked at the numbers on the doors to get a clue as to where to go. Once they had a direction in mind, they wished each other luck and separated down the busy hallway of ninth graders frantically searching for their own homerooms.

CHAPTER 1

Brandi

Brandi was still looking for her homeroom when she heard someone calling her name. She turned around and was greeted by the captain of the cheerleading squad, Alexandria Solis. "Hey, lady! You look lost," Alex said. Alex's dark black hair made her look exotic. She had a look that other girls envied, and she knew how to flaunt it.

"Yeah, well, this school is huge and confusing. What are you doing over here in the ninth-grade wing?" Brandi asked.

"Had to come find my freshmen cheer girls and make sure y'all were taken care of. Have you seen Adrian or Melody anywhere?"

"Nope, you are the first one I've seen from the squad so far. There were so many people in the cafeteria."

"Maybe they found their way already. Let's find out where you have to be."

"Good idea! I am looking for ten-A."

To Brandi's surprise, Alex pointed to the door they were standing in front of and both girls laughed. Alex patted Brandi on the back and said, "Well, I'll see you at practice. Meet us at the girls' gym at three forty-five and don't be late. Now you do know your way to the gym, right?" she asked playfully.

"Ha-ha," Brandi said sarcastically. "Now *that* I can find!" she yelled as Alex disappeared down the hallway.

Brandi was one of the last people in class. *Why am I always so late? Well, it's the perfect opportunity to make an entrance, at least that's what Shane always says,* she thought. *Her mind was racing. I hope I don't have a wedgie ... I didn't get to check my teeth ... I should have gone to the restroom ... Where can I sit? ... Who should I sit by? ... Oh, just make a decision, Brandi!* She finally located a chair near the front of the class but not in the front row.

Just as she sat down, she thought about Matthew and wondered how he was fairing in high school. Matthew Kincade was Brandi's ex-boyfriend from junior high. She couldn't stand that she was thinking of him after what he had done to her this summer while she was away at cheerleading camp. She had invested so much of herself in their relationship, and he threw it all away. He wasn't even worth her anger. *Boo on you, Matthew,* she thought.

The rest of the day was typical for any first day of school: super boring. The only thing Brandi looked forward to was seeing the other cheerleaders at practice that afternoon. She may not have known her way around campus, but she could have located the gym with her eyes closed. Two-a-days had kicked her butt for a month before school started. It seemed like all her summer had consisted of was practice, practice, practice ... prepare for camp, prepare for the first pep rally, prepare for the first game. She loved every minute of it. It took her mind off of her home life. Brandi's parents had been arguing for forever now, and cheerleading was her escape.

As soon as Brandi entered the gym, she headed straight to the locker room. Once all the girls were done putting on their practice outfits, they started the one-mile run around the school. Brandi was chatting with Christina Hall during their run. She was a sophomore and Brandi's closest friend on the squad. Brandi had been Christina's roommate during cheerleading camp at a time when Christina could really use a friend. Christina had been outcasted by the other cheerleaders for saying that she didn't see what the big fuss was over Alexandria. It was a simple statement, but it didn't sit well with Alex. Brandi had been the only person brave enough to step up and be Christina's roommate. The other girls got mad at Brandi too, but they secretly wished that they could have been strong enough to stand up to the whole squad. By the time school started, the pettiness had been put behind them, but Brandi and Christina's bond was still there. "So, did you see Matthew today?" Christina asked.

"Nah, I'm not sweating Matthew at all this year. I am soooo over him."

"Really?" Christina asked, surprised. "So you didn't talk to him at all? That's so crazy."

"Not really. That chapter is closed."

There was somebody on the football team that Brandi had been eyeing all summer. He was extremely fine, but she hadn't told anybody that she was crushing on him. Not even Marisa or Shane knew. She didn't even know his name to tell anybody. Plus, he was a junior. He probably already had a girlfriend. She was sure she didn't stand a chance.

Just as the girls turned the corner by the cafeteria, the football team was heading to the practice field. That's when it happened. She came so close to Crush—as she had labeled him in her head—that she was sure she could smell his cologne. *Omigod, Omigod! I can't look directly at him, just keep running!* she told herself.

When Crush passed by her, he gave her a nod and said, "Hey, Brandi."

How did he know my name? she wondered. *Was he talking to me? What just happened?*

With her mind spinning, she tripped over absolutely nothing at all and felt more embarrassed than she had in her entire life. Some of the other football players saw her and laughed. "You okay, fish?" a couple of them hollered.

"Watch out for the air, it's dangerous," one laughed.

"Girl, are you okay?" Christina asked. "Looks like Brendon has you shook," she said with a laugh.

"Oh, bite me, Chris!" she paused. "What's his name again?"

"Uh-huh, no wonder Matthew's a closed chapter. Looks like a new chapter might be in the works, huh?"

"Girl, I just want to know his name so if he speaks to me again, I can respond. I don't want to be rude and clumsy," she joked.

"Yeah, tell me anything. Just send me an invitation to the wedding," Christina joked as they finished up their run.

Alexandria addressed the girls about the upcoming game on Friday. There were three freshmen on the squad, and this was new to all of them. As Alexandria began to break down Friday's schedule, Brandi could feel the adrenaline move through her body from the anticipation of cheering at her first high school game.

Then her thoughts drifted to her parents. Would they be there to support her? She didn't think so. They never showed up to any of her junior high activities. Why would high school be any different?

CHAPTER 2

Marisa

When Marisa arrived in homeroom, she took a seat and waited patiently. She looked around for familiar faces. Then the guy next to her said, "Hey, Mari, did you have a good summer?"

"Oh, hey, Matt," she said, smiling. "I didn't even notice you were sitting there. My summer was fun ... lots of practicing to get our twirling routines ready for football season. But I guess I'm preaching to the choir. You probably practiced way more than I did." Matthew played running back for Port City High, and though he was a freshman, they were considering moving him to varsity. It was all the buzz in the freshman class.

"Yeah, high school is a lot of work already and today's only the first day. What's your schedule looking like? Did you get anything interesting?" he asked. They exchanged schedules and realized that they were very similar. "Looks like we'll be seeing a lot of each other this school year," Matthew pointed out.

"I'm just glad that somebody I know is in my classes. That'll be cool. Have you seen Brandi at all?"

"Nah, I haven't talked to Brandi in ages. You know how Brandi is … she doesn't want to hear anything I have to say anymore."

"Well, I think that she has a good reason for feeling that way," Marisa responded, rolling her eyes. "Oh, wow … I shouldn't have said that. That's between y'all."

"Nah, it's all good, Mari. I wouldn't expect anything else from you but honesty.

I know I messed up. I learned a huge lesson, though. I'll never cheat on another female. The price is too high."

"Good!" Just then they heard the bell ring, signaling the transition to first period. The two of them strolled down the hallway to their next class.

During lunch, Marisa looked around to see if she could find Brandi and Shane, but they were nowhere to be found. *This sucks!* she thought. *They must have second lunch.*

Suddenly she saw Ashley and her crew coming toward her. "Hey, Marisa," snorted one of Ashley's little minions.

"Hey," she responded back, trying to hide her disdain. "*Que paso*, Ashley?"

"*Nada, chica.* How are you fairing in the big pond? Where's your crew? I ain't never seen you fly solo before."

"I think they have second lunch. Thanks for your concern," she retorted sarcastically.

"Ooh, well, you're more than welcome to join us for lunch."

Just then, Marisa spotted Matthew sitting with his homies. He was waving her over to his table. "Thanks, but I'm gonna pass. I see somebody I need to talk to."

Ashley asked, "Who, Matthew? I saw y'all walking together a lot today. It's a shame not to have loyalty within a group. I'd never be crushing on one of my besties' exes."

"Whoa, hold on, Ashley. What are you accusing me of? Seriously, you have been pathetic since elementary school. I thought you might have grown up since then."

"Yeah, explain that to Brandi when she sees you and her precious Mattie getting all chummy."

"Girl, Brandi ain't tripping on Matt and neither am I."

"Who are you trying to convince? Me? Or you?"

"Bite me, Ashley! Get a life." Mari turned to go and eat with Matt and his crew.

Ashley was always trying to stir the pot. She would do anything to make Mari's life miserable. She'd been jealous of Marisa, Brandi, and Shane's friendship since the fourth grade. All four girls had gone to grade school together but were thankfully separated during junior high. Ashley went to Washington Junior High and was able to gain status that would have been unreachable if Marisa, Brandi, or Shane had gone there.

Deep down, Ashley knew that when they were around, she lived in their shadow. She would do or say anything to break up their friendship. She seemed to especially have it out for Marisa. Maybe it was because they were both Hispanic. Or maybe it was because they had been really close at one point. Whatever the reason, Marisa hated being around her. It always meant trouble.

"What was that about?" Matt asked.

"Nothing ... you know Ashley. Always tryna start drama." Marisa hoped that Ashley would just drop it. She was kind of enjoying Matt's company. They had been friends for a long time too. Knowing that she would never do anything to hurt her friendship with Brandi, she wasn't too worried about hanging out with Matt. They had almost all of their classes together; it'd be weird to not hang out, but she didn't want to give anybody the wrong idea. Hopefully Brandi would understand, and they could laugh in Ashley's face together.

CHAPTER 3

Shane

Shane arrived at her homeroom without getting lost. Once again she was fashionably late and loving it. Making an entrance never bothered Shane. She loved hanging out with her girls, but rolling solo was nice sometimes. As she walked through the door, she tossed her freshly flat-ironed hair and had an I-have-arrived-you-may-now-begin smirk on her face.

The first person who caught her eye was Riley. She sat next to her, and they started catching up on their summers. Shane hadn't seen Riley in the three months they had been out of school. Riley was Shane's buddy from junior high. They were always ready to break the rules: skipping school to hit up the movie theater, smoking weed under the bleachers, or flirting with boys just for the fun of it. They had some good times together, but Shane was determined to turn over a new leaf this year.

Once the teacher passed out their schedules, Riley turned to Shane. "Hey, you wanna go hit a little (she whistled) before we go to first period?" she asked.

Oh, that sounds so good, Shane thought, but she declined. "Girl, I can't. I don't wanna go to class on the first day smelling like a pound. Not only that, but I haven't smoked since the last day of school. I'd be too high to function."

"Since the last day of school?! What, you been hospitalized?" Riley joked.

"Nah, just trying to get my life together. I feel like that was Junior High Shane, and this is High School Shane. Just being here is making me high."

"All right, let me know when you wanna get down and we will."

They dapped each other up and headed off to first period.

Shane's day was pretty boring until she got to fifth period. She had enrolled in journalism for one of her electives. She knew she would be writing for the school newspaper. But she didn't know what else to expect since journalism wasn't offered in junior high. *I hope this class is going to be super fun*, thought Shane.

Mrs. Monroe announced that she would be putting together the yearbook committee and that she wanted each student to think about being a part of it. Shane knew that it was right up her alley, so she raised her hand and told Mrs. Monroe to sign her up.

After class Mrs. Monroe pulled Shane aside and told her she was excited about her being a part of the committee. She asked Shane if she would head up the freshmen section, saying that she trusted Shane with the task and knew she would do a great job. Shane was all over it. Not only would she get to write, but she would also be in charge of approving the articles and pictures that went in the yearbook.

Shane had so many ideas about how to make the yearbook great. After school she went to the library to look at yearbooks from previous years so that she could see what worked and what didn't. She wanted to get an early start and make sure her class would be represented to the fullest.

CHAPTER 4

The Dance

This was the girls' first Friday night in high school. They planned to meet up after the game and sleep over at Shane's house. The worst part about this year was that they barely had any classes together, so the weekends were important. It was their time to unwind and catch up on the events of the week.

The game was hectic! There was so much to do. Brandi was cheering, Marisa was twirling, and Shane was taking pictures for the school newspaper, with the future yearbook also in mind. She walked around with her camera draped around her neck and a notepad and pencil in her pocket. She spotted Brandi and snapped pictures of her and Christina, both smiling in their uniforms. Shane liked Christina and was happy that she was there for Brandi on the squad. She knew that cheerleaders could get pretty nasty with each other, and since she sure wasn't into cheering, Brandi was on her own.

Then Shane tried looking for Marisa, who was somewhere amidst the huge band, flag girls, and twirlers. It was pure mayhem in the stands. The Wildcats had just scored a touchdown, and the crowd was going wild. Shane snapped away, getting several shots that she deemed perfect for this week's newspaper. She finally spotted Marisa and snapped a few of her. *My girls are going to be front page whenever possible*, Shane thought. She didn't need to have her face all over anything as long as her name was attached to the photograph.

After the game Shane turned in her camera to Mrs. Monroe. Then she sent a text to the girls to let them know her sister was in the parking lot to pick them up. Even though Robin was a senior, she hung out with the girls from time to time, mainly when they needed rides. The girls piled into the car, and once again they were on their high school high.

"The game was awesome!" Marisa announced. "Did you get any pictures of me on the field during halftime, Shane?"

"Now you know I did! Gots to make sure we stay on their minds."

"Girl, I am so happy you're doing the school newspaper and the yearbook. It can't get much better! I'm about to see my beautiful face er'where," she said, grooving to the hot new track from the newest rapper in Texas, Young Dub.

"No, no, no," corrected Brandi, "we're going to see *our* beautiful faces er'where!" They danced, laughed, and sang all the way to Shane's house and kept the fun going while they got dressed for the back-to-school party at the Room. The Room was the hottest spot in the area that allowed people under eighteen. The DJ mixed in new school and old school jams so you never knew what they were going to play.

It was going to be packed. Anybody who was somebody was going to be at the Room. Dress code gone, uniforms gone ... it was all about their own swag, and the girls knew how to represent. They decided tonight was a little-black-dress night. They had gone shopping before school even started to make sure they would look extra hot.

When they walked into the party, it was like the music stopped. All eyes were on them, which seemed to piss off some of the other girls—sophomores, juniors, and seniors alike. They were the new girls on the block, and they were about to get it hot! Of course, nobody was bad enough to call them on it. Nobody except Ashley.

Unbeknownst to them, Ashley and her minions were actually in line behind them. "Um, excuse me," Ashley said, tapping Marisa on the shoulder.

"I know she didn't just touch me," Marisa said.

"Yeah, I did. You and your hoochie crew are in our way."

At that point, Shane stepped in to break up what looked to be the start of yet another battle between Ashley and Marisa. "Mari, don't let *butter face* ruin our night."

"Butter face?" sneered Ashley.

"Girl, I know you've heard that before, er'thing cute. But. Her. Face!"

The girls laughed hysterically and walked to the restroom to check their look.

Brandi asked, "Why do you let Ashley get to you? Y'all have been beefin' since fourth grade. I mean, I don't like her either, but she knows she can get to you, so she tries to push your buttons every time."

"I guess it's because we used to be friends. I don't know, but I ain't trippin' on the ole girl tonight. I need to see what's poppin'," Marisa responded, dancing in the mirror to the beat that had the whole restroom vibrating. "Let's see what's good!"

The girls took one last look in the mirror and struck their best pose. Brandi snapped a picture with her cell. Priceless!

When they walked out of the restroom, it seemed that all the other girls were looking at them. They gave their best we-don't-care-if-you-hate faces and fell into the crowd. While they were walking, Brandi felt somebody grab her hand. She turned to see who it was and saw Brendon staring down at her. "Yo, Brandi. I know ya gonna save a dance for me tonight," he said.

Brandi nearly passed out. She felt like her heart dropped to her stomach. She managed to stay cool this time. "And you are?" she asked, pretending that she hadn't been sweating him.

Brendon grinned, "Oh, my bad. I'm Brendon."

"Well, Brendon ... find me later."

"Bet!" he said, dapping up one of his friends.

The girls worked their way through the crowd to get to the Nook, where you could buy gum, water, sodas, and snacks. They ordered three bottles of water and decided to post up for a minute. Matthew spotted them and came over.

"Yo, y'all are getting it hot up in here. Seems like the whole football team is sweating you three," he said. This was Brandi and Matthew's first time talking since the breakup. Brandi wasn't feeling friendly, but she also wasn't one to cause a scene.

"Aww, Mattie. You know we gotta keep 'em on their toes," Shane said.

Matthew asked Marisa and Shane if he could get a second to holler at Brandi. Brandi rolled her eyes, but she told the girls it was okay and that she would find them later.

"What, Matt?"

"Dang, girl, I just wanted to say hi. We haven't spoken since—"

"And that's the way I want to keep it, Matthew."

"That's not right, B. You know we've been through too much to go out like that. I know we can find some way to stay friends," he smiled playfully and hugged her. Brandi's anger melted away, and she knew she couldn't stay mad at him.

"Okay, but only friends. That's all we'll ever be."

Just then they heard their song starting to play ... *What I need from you is understaaaanding* ... Matthew looked at her and said, "Come on, one last dance."

"Why not?" she replied, and they walked to the dance floor. They held each other through the first verse, just like old times.

Brendon was watching the whole scene from afar and decided that it was time to move in for the kill. He had heard that Brandi and Matt weren't dating anymore, so he figured he'd better break up this little party before it went too far.

"Hey, li'l dude, mind if I cut in?" he asked.

Matt was just about to shoo him away when Brandi answered for him and said, "It's okay." He took a step back and gestured for Brendon to cut in. It hurt to hand her over to someone else, but he knew he had to let her go. He had ruined their relationship, and he wanted someone to make her happy. He couldn't do that anymore, but maybe Brendon could.

When Matt walked away, he saw Marisa and went over to her. "Hey, Mari. Well, that was *not* easy."

"What happened?"

"I was dancing with B and that kid Brendon cut in on our song. I was about to say nah, but Brandi said it was cool. So I just bounced. I know the deal, but that doesn't make it any easier."

"I'm surprised she even danced with you. Brandi's getting soft in her old age." They both laughed.

At that moment, Brandi was dancing with Brendon; she enjoyed being in his arms. They were about to pull away as the song ended when "Weak" by SWV played loudly through the sound system. It was like the DJ had read Brandi's thoughts: she was weak and enjoying every minute of it. Brendon had that effect on her, and it was scary.

At two in the morning, the lights flicked on and off. The girls were separated in different directions, but they had a plan to meet by the Nook if they weren't together when it was closing time. Brandi was still chillin' with Brendon, and he invited all of them to join him and his friends at Waffle House on him. They walked over to the Nook, where Marisa and Shane were waiting.

Brandi introduced Brendon to Marisa and Shane, and Brendon asked the girls if they were feeling Waffle House. Shane said, "Let me see what Robin says." Robin was their ride after the club, so she hit her up on the cell. "Hey, Robie, you feel like going to Waffle House? ... Cool. We'll be out front." She hung up. "Yeah, she's down."

They almost had more fun at Waffle House than they had at the Room. Brendon's friends were awesome, and they all just clicked immediately. They laughed and talked till they could barely keep their eyes open.

They stayed out until four. That was the cool thing about staying at Shane's house: her parents didn't give her or Robin a curfew. They just trusted them.

It had been a long day: first school, then their victory over the Bulldogs, then the party, then Waffle House, and now ... sleep.

CHAPTER 5

Marisa

As Mrs. Sumner explained the criteria for their science projects, Marisa was already planning out how she and Matt were going to tackle the assignment. "Man, the other science classes don't even start on their projects for another month. Brandi and Shane both have Coach Walters. I wish I did," Marisa said to Matt, who looked like he was in another world.

"Yeah," Matt responded dryly.

"And I was thinking that after school I would go take a hike down Sarah Jane

Highway to see if I can catch her ghost. What do you think about that?"

"Sounds cool."

She hit him on the arm. "Matt, what's wrong with you? Are you listening to me at all?"

Mrs. Sumner cleared her throat. Marisa looked up to see their teacher staring at her. She would figure out what was going on with Matt later. Once Mrs. Sumner finished with the directions and they had gone over the grading procedure for their project, Marisa turned to Matt. "What's going on? Did somebody steal your bike?" she joked, trying to make light of his heavy mood.

Matt looked at Marisa and said, "Mari, just focus on the project and not on me."

Wow ... I wasn't expecting that ... she thought. "Sorry, Mattie ... I was just trying to help," she said.

"Dang, I'm sorry. I shouldn't have snapped at you like that. It's just ..."

"Is it B? It's because of her and Brendon, huh?"

He almost laughed out loud, "Girl, no ... I'm *so* past that. It's my parents. They've been fighting a lot lately, but last night got really heated. I even heard them talk about a divorce. I think that it's inevitable."

Marisa wasn't prepared to advise Matt on his parents' problems. She had never experienced anything like that. "Maybe you should talk to Brandi, Matt. I know that she's been through a similar situation with her parents."

"Nah, B's doing her own thing right now. I'ma let her make it."

"Is there anything I can do?"

They were so deep in their conversation that they didn't even realize Mrs. Sumner was standing behind them. "Matthew, Marisa, I would rather not assign detention for you two. You already have enough activities after school. Please get on task."

"Yes, ma'am," Marisa responded. "Okay, let's finish this later," she whispered to Matt.

"You think we could meet up after practice? We could grab a burger. I'll treat," he responded in hushed tones.

"Sure, but you don't have to pay. It's on me."

As soon as Matt was done with football practice, he went to look for Marisa at the meet spot. He pulled up next to her and said, "Get in, girl."

"What are you doing driving? We aren't even old enough for permits yet."

"Yeah, well, one good thing about my parents stressing over each other is that nobody's stressing over me. So get in, I'm starving."

They headed over to Jerry's to grab a bite to eat. Jerry's was a cute restaurant where you could get a huge homemade burger and fries for a very reasonable price. It was a great place for students to get the most for their money. After they ordered and sat down, Matt let out a heavy sigh. "Now that we're here, I don't even wanna talk about my parents. I'd rather just forget about it. Talking ain't gonna fix it anyway."

"Hey, nobody said you have to talk about it," Marisa responded.

"Number forty-five?" they heard over the intercom. "Number forty-five!"

"That's us. I'll grab it," Matt said.

When he got up to get the food, Brandi and Brendon walked through the door holding hands. When Brandi saw Marisa, she dropped Brendon's hand and ran over to the table. "Marisa! I'm so glad you're here. Hey, we're going to order and come join you. Are you here with Shane? Where is she?" Before she could finish her sentence, she saw Matt walking toward her with their food. "Oh ..." she said.

"Hey, B," Matt said, oblivious to the awkwardness that accompanied his arrival. "What's up, Brendon? Y'all wanna join us?"

Brendon noticed that Brandi was feeling uncomfortable and answered for her, "Nah, we were taking ours to go. I know about this great spot that I wanna take Brandi to. It was supposed to be a surprise, but it's all good."

"I'll catch up with you later, Mari," Brandi said.

"B?"

"Hey, we'll talk later. No worries." Marisa appreciated Brandi not making a big deal out of her dinner with Matt. She knew Brandi was pissed. But after she explained the situation with Matt's parents, she knew Brandi would understand. After all, Brandi was once very close to them.

When Matt and Marisa finished their food, they jumped in the car and headed home. When they pulled up in Marisa's driveway, they both just sat. Matt said, "I don't even wanna go home. Thanks for coming out with me, Mari. This was nice."

Marisa was content just sitting too. She was enjoying Matt's company. He had always been like one of her girlfriends, and she hadn't been able to hang out with Shane and Brandi in a while. It was nice to have somebody to clown around with, even though his mood was changing constantly.

"I have to go before my parents start blowing up my cell. I'll see you in the morning," said Marisa as she rounded up her belongings. "Have you seen my phone? I can't find it anywhere." They searched in the back seat and on the floor but they couldn't find it. Matt felt under his seat, and there it was.

"Here!" he started to say, but when he came up, they were inches apart from each other.

"Um ... thanks. I'd better go," she said in a voice that she didn't recognize. Something wouldn't let her turn away. She tried to force her hand to the door but couldn't. When she finally mustered up the strength, it was too late. They had kissed. He didn't kiss her, she didn't kiss him, they kissed each other.

"I gotta go," Marisa whispered as she hurried out of the car.

"Mari!" he hollered. She turned back but knew there was nothing more to say.

CHAPTER 6

Brandi

Brandi's attitude was a bit solemn. Brendon was talking to her as he drove to an undisclosed location. "Earth to Brandi ... hey, it's okay."

"What?" she asked.

"It's okay. I know you're upset about seeing Marisa with Matthew."

"I am *not* upset about seeing Marisa with Matthew, Brendon. Don't pretend that you know me better than you do," she spat.

"Whoa, you don't have to get mad at me. I'm not the one having dinner with your best friend. That would be your ex-boyfriend. It's all right for you to be upset."

"Number one, Brendon, I don't need your permission to be upset. And number two, I'm not upset! Mari is my best friend. I'm sure there's a good explanation for it. They have a lot of classes together this year. We have all been friends for a really long time."

"Brandi, you don't have to convince me of anything. And this isn't what I had in mind for tonight. I was the one who had your back in there, and now you're taking this out on me. Maybe we should just call it a night."

"Fine by me," Brandi shot back. She couldn't believe she was allowing Matt to ruin her night with Brendon. He had already ruined her summer, and now she was letting him ruin her date. *How pathetic!* she thought. If anybody else had been sitting at the table with Mattie, she wouldn't be angry right now. But it was

Mari. She was so confused that her head was spinning.

Brendon had been able to see through her hard demeanor. He knew that she was angry about seeing them together, which enraged her even more. *What would he think?* she thought. She would have to deal with him later. Right now she had to go home and make sense of the night's events.

Brendon pulled up to her house. "Don't forget your food," he said dryly.

"Brendon, I'm sorry," she said, but that was all she had. She didn't even know how she felt. How could she explain it to him?

As soon as she walked in the house, she called Shane. She couldn't talk to Marisa right now. She just wasn't in the mood. Shane would know what was going on. "Shane? You busy?"

"Girl, no. I was just trying to stay awake. I have an article due tomorrow, but I'm having writer's block mixed with sleepiness, and it's proving to be harder than I thought."

"Oh—"

"Uh-oh, what's wrong?"

"Nothing. Something. Well, I'll explain." She told her how she had run into Marisa having dinner with Matt at Jerry's and how she had taken it out on Brendon. She told her how confused she was about her feelings. Shane had been silent through the whole conversation.

"Shane ... you there?"

"Yeah, I'm here, B. I was just listening."

"So, what do you think?

"Well, first you need to talk to Marisa. You know Mari, she wouldn't do anything to hurt you. And second, you need to do some kissing up to Brendon. You were so wrong. The boy was just trying to be there for you."

"I know. I know."

"Call me when you get all of this figured out. I'll be right here trying to put some words on this blank sheet of paper in front of me."

"Will do!" When she hung up the phone, she called Marisa. She didn't get an answer. It was almost eight o'clock. Was it possible that she was still out with Matt? No ... she wouldn't be.

Thirty minutes later, her phone rang. *All the single ladies, all the single ladies* blared. She automatically knew it was Mari. It was her ring. "Hey, Mari."

"Hey, Brandi! I misplaced my phone. That's why it took me so long to get back at you."

"Oh ... I figured you were still out with Matt."

"Girl, no," she lied. She couldn't tell her about kissing Matt. The last thing she wanted to do was hurt Brandi. But if she found out from somebody else, she would be even more hurt. *Tell her now*, she thought, but she didn't. "Matt was really upset in class today. I told him he should talk to you, but he didn't want to bother you. His parents are talking about getting a divorce."

"No! Are you serious? I love the Kincades. Matt could have talked to me. You know my parents have been on the brink of divorce forever. Somehow, they always manage to put things back together."

"That's why I told him he should talk to you." Brandi felt so bad for thinking that something was going on between Marisa and Matt. How could she? After all, Mari was her best friend.

CHAPTER 7

Shane

I have to focus and get this article together. Mrs. Monroe is going to expect something really great, and I just can't let her down, Shane thought. Lately it had been increasingly difficult to stay awake. Usually she could breeze through an article, but right now she just wanted to sleep. She decided to take a break and went outside to sit on the porch. It was a nice night. Fall in Texas could be so calming. There was no humidity that night, and the mosquitoes seemed to be on vacation. She was straight chillin'.

Shane closed her eyes and dozed off for a second. She was awakened by her cell phone vibrating angrily on the swing next to her.

"What up?" It was Riley.

"Girl, nothing ... just trying to get this article together. What'cha doing? Working on yours?"

"Girl, no. I'm done. I mixed a little bit of this with a little bit of that and *voilá*."

"What are you rambling about?"

"One of my friends turned me on to this pill that cuts my appetite and gives me energy."

"Is it a diet pill? My mom says that she's on something like that, but she told me it's not for kids. She's wack."

"Something like that. It's for kids with ADHD; calms them down. But if you don't have ADHD, it has the opposite effect"

"Oh, that can't be too bad. Seems like half of our class is getting called to the office to pop their meds during the day."

"You can try one if you want. But not at night because you'll never sleep."

"I doubt it. I'm passing out right now. Maybe I could try half a pill just to get through this article tonight."

"Cool! Fall through. I'm at the house now."

Shane took the all too familiar walk to Riley's house. In eighth grade she would head over there to smoke a little something before bed. Tonight she was going to get something to make her stay up. She was super stressed over this stupid article.

She sent Riley a text, "b der n 2 mins."

Riley answered, "com round bak."

Before she could get to the back porch, she could smell the weed burning. It smelled good. She had to be strong. She had so much going for her, and she didn't want to blow it. No pun intended. "Hey, Riley."

Riley extended her arm that held the blunt. "Want a hit?"

"Oh maaaan ... why not?" she said, giving in much quicker than she expected. "I need to relieve some of this stress. It'll probably help me focus."

"I'ma tell you ... once you take this pill, you'll be focused. I already split one for you. Here, half now, half later."

Shane took the halved pill from Riley and popped it in her mouth. She hoped she wouldn't regret taking it so late. She puffed on the blunt and exhaled. "Now I see what you meant about a little bit of this with a little bit of that," she laughed.

"Girl, you know how I do it. I just hate that you're taking this pill at night. You may be up for a while."

"It's all good. It's almost the weekend, so I'll catch up on sleep then. You got snacks? I think I have the munchies. I haven't had weed in so long."

Riley passed her a munchies box, and the girls sat and talked for another half hour. "Keep the munchies box, you may need it," Riley said. "I put some more pills in there for you too."

By that time Shane could feel the pill starting to kick in. She headed back home to get some work done and work she did. She finished the article, cleaned the kitchen, cleaned her room, wrapped her hair, and ironed her clothes. It was one in the morning but she still couldn't sleep.

She went on Facebook and then Friender to see who was online. She stayed on the computer until all of her friends went to bed. At two thirty she was still up ... *I will never sleep again*, she thought. *Maybe I should just lie in bed.*

At three thirty, she opened up the munchies box to get a snack; she was just bored, not hungry. She saw a blunt in the box already rolled with a note that said, "Just in case."

She laughed. "Thank you, Riley," she said aloud.

Shane snuck out to the back porch and lit the blunt. *Finally, I will be able to sleep,* she thought. She sat there and smoked the whole blunt by herself. By the time it was over, she was in pretty bad shape. She stumbled back into the house, happy that she hadn't run into her parents or Robin. She knew that she smelled like a pound of weed. At that point, the only thing she could do was go to bed. It didn't take long before she dozed off.

When she woke up, something felt wrong. She looked at the clock. "Shoot!" She had overslept, but she still had time to get her flash drive to Mrs. Monroe before the deadline. She got dressed as fast as she could. It was a good thing she had wrapped her hair and ironed her clothes the night before. She brushed her teeth and hurried out the door.

As soon as she got to school, she went straight to her journalism class and nervously handed her flash drive to Mrs. Monroe. Mrs. Monroe stopped her class to accept the article from Shane. "You had me worried; we almost had to go to press without your article."

"I am so sorry, Mrs. Monroe. It'll never happen again. I had a rough night."

"It happens, but, Shane ... don't let it happen again. I'm counting on you. I have to be able to trust you."

"You can, Mrs. Monroe. I promise." What a close call. Shane knew that all of her efforts the night before to get the article finished had almost been useless. She went to the office to get her pass to her first class and vowed that she wouldn't let herself fall into a situation like that again. She just couldn't.

CHAPTER 8

Strange Behavior

*I*t was homecoming week, so Port City High School was filled with corsages, teddy bears, cookie cakes, and banners. The whole school was on a high school high. Everybody was in preparation mode. Every day there was something to do: mix and match day, hat day, bowling night, pizza night, and game night. The homecoming dance was going to be Saturday night. This was how high school was supposed to be.

After the game on Friday, the girls were spending the night at Shane's in preparation for Saturday's big shopping day. They had to be ready for the homecoming dance. Brandi and Brendon were going to the dance together. Shane had to work for the school newspaper, so she didn't even sweat not having a date. And Marisa was going to ride with some of the other twirlers. The girls weren't going to the dance together, so they wanted to make the most of what they referred to as their "getting ready time." Robin had agreed to help them with everything: nails, eyebrows, lashes, hair, clothes, makeup ... the works.

That night they memorized the words to a few of their favorite songs, sang along with them, harmonized, danced, and just had a great time. The clock was ticking, though, and it had been a long day. The homecoming game was awesome, but they needed to get some sleep if they were going to tackle the upcoming day.

Brandi yawned, "I'm about to lay it down for the night. I'm beat."

"Me too," replied Marisa.

"Y'all are some party poopers. I was just getting started," Shane responded.

"Girl, you need to get some sleep too. I saw you running up and down those bleachers, snapping pictures during the game. If you get some sleep, you may be able to get rid of those dark circles under your eyes," Brandi said.

"Dark circles?" Shane asked, looking in the mirror. *Wow, my eyes are looking dark*, she thought. *I wonder if it's those pills I'm popping. Nah.* "I probably need to drink more water," she said.

"Yeah, and get some sleep," Marisa noted.

"You're right," she said to get the girls off her back. "Let's just lay it down for the night."

Marisa and Brandi fell asleep without any problems. It seemed like it took them all of two minutes. Shane, on the other hand, was lying on the bed and staring at the ceiling. She just couldn't sleep. Those pills gave her a lot of energy, but she couldn't shake them off at bedtime. It was really frustrating, but she couldn't get everything done without taking them.

Shane tried to fight the urge to smoke a blunt, but she couldn't. She snuck out to the back porch and fired up. *Ahhh*, she thought, *that should do it.*

The girls woke up the next morning, but Shane would not get out of the bed. "Shane, you're ruining our plans. Get up so we can get started. We're going to miss our nail appointments!" cried Marisa.

"Dang! Leave me alone! I couldn't sleep last night," yelled Shane. Her mood was getting erratic. It was so hard for her to control her emotions. She tried to calm down once she realized that she startled Marisa. One part of her cared, but the other part thought, *get over it!*

Brandi yelled, "Shane! What's wrong with you? You need to calm down."

"You're yelling at me! *You* need to calm down." This was not how Shane wanted to start the day. She stormed off into the bathroom to separate herself from the situation and leaned against the door. *I'm just tired … I'm just tired …* she thought. She splashed water on her face, popped her little pill, brushed her teeth, and left the bathroom.

When she entered her room, the girls were nowhere to be found. She assumed they had left until she heard voices coming from Robin's room.

"She's just under a lot of pressure right now, y'all. She's taking her journalism job to heart. She sees it as her ticket out of here. Just give her a break."

"I don't care," Brandi said. "That's no way to treat your friends."

"You are right," Shane said as she entered her sister's room. "Marisa, I'm sorry. Do y'all still wanna hang out today?"

"You know I can't stay mad at you, Shane," Marisa said and hugged her neck.

"I can!" responded Brandi with a smile. "But I won't … this time."

"Okay, then let's get moving! I'll drop y'all off at the mall," Robin said.

The girls spent the entire day at the mall. Thankfully they had made their nail appointments months in advance, so they were in and out of the salon. The other girls seemed to be waiting forever, but not them. After the salon, they found their outfits and headed to lunch. They had to choose between Jason's Deli and Casa Olé.

"That queso is gonna go straight to our bellies, and we have to fit in those little dresses we bought," Brandi said.

"True. I think Jason's Deli would be our best bet. Then we can munch on salad," Shane responded.

"Sounds like a plan. I don't want to look like a stuffed turkey. I have to look good for Brendon."

The girls had such a good time at the mall. Their excitement had been building for the upcoming evening. When they went back to Shane's house, they packed their belongings, then headed home to shower and get dressed for their first high school homecoming dance.

CHAPTER 9

Marisa

Marisa was so excited for homecoming. She was happy she didn't have a date. Dates could be such a headache. What made it even better was that some of the other twirlers decided to go solo too. She heard the horn outside and ran to the door. "*Mami*, I'm leaving!" she yelled.

"*Esperas, esperas!*" her mother yelled, running to the front of the house with her camera.

"English, Mama!" Marisa said, scolding her mother. She was trying to get her mother to speak more English. After years of being in America, her English communication skills were still lacking.

"Okay, wait for your father. I want to take your picture with him."

"The girls are waiting, Mama. Tell *Papi* to hurry."

"He's coming, *mi hija*. Nadia!" she yelled for Marisa's little sister. "Come take our picture."

Beep, beep. "Mama, the girls ..." Marisa whined. She flashed the porch light off and on to let them know she was coming. Her father and Nadia came running to the front at the same time.

"You look beautiful," her father said proudly. They snapped pictures and Marisa bolted out the door.

"Sorry. My parents wanted to take pictures at the last minute."

"No worries. Our families did the same thing. That's why we're so late. You look adorable!" Hayley told her as she climbed in the SUV. Hayley Brooks was the feature twirler at Port City High. Halftime during football season was her show. She had a solo at every game. One week she twirled three batons, the next week hoops, the next week flags, and for homecoming she twirled fire. She always put on a spectacular show. There were even rumors that she would be competing for the next Miss Texas title.

The twirlers for PCH all had model-like bodies. They were tall and thin, unlike the cheerleaders who were shorter and more curvaceous. Everyone told Marisa that she should be a model. She planned on trying her hand at it once she graduated from high school.

"Thanks, Hayley. What's up, ladies? Y'all ready to turn the party out?"

"You know we are," they chimed. Each of the girls looked beautiful. They arrived in Hayley's mom's Suburban that had just enough room to fit them all. When they turned into the parking lot, they cranked the music up. Heads turned in their direction. *What a way to make an entrance*, thought Marisa. She was hanging with the upperclassmen, and this was how they rolled.

Hayley made a call. "Meet us out front," she said. When they pulled up to the drop-off line, there were five guys waiting. Hayley said, "Let's be off this!"

"But wait ... aren't we gonna park?" Marisa asked.

All of a sudden her door swung open. Standing at each door were four guys from the nearby college. Hayley handed the keys to a fifth guy. They were gorgeous and looked super mature. They each wore a red and white jacket that said Kappa Alpha Psi. Marisa did not expect this at all. She was stunned. The guys looked like Greek gods as they escorted each of the girls to the door. They kissed the girls' hands and said, "See you at two."

Marisa didn't want to seem immature, but that blew her away. "Hayley ... you should have warned me. That was crazy! How much did you pay them?"

"Girl, I didn't pay them," she laughed. "Those are some of my big brothers. They take care of me and my girls." She winked. Marisa didn't know what to say. They were so hot. For a moment she wished that she was about to graduate and go off to college too. But she had just started her high school career, and she was going to enjoy every minute of it.

Once they were in the dance, they went straight to the restroom to freshen up. "Okay, ladies, not a hair out of place," Hayley instructed. "We have to look better than our best. We have to look *the* best." Once the girls had the stamp of approval from Hayley, they took pictures and headed out to the dance.

The first person Marisa saw when she entered the dance was Matthew. *Dang, he's everywhere*, she thought. He was there with his date, a cute freshman who went to Washington Junior High the previous year. Marisa had seen her around but didn't really know her.

When Matthew spotted Marisa, he walked over to her. "Hey, Mari," he said, smiling.

"Hey, Matt. Have you seen Shane and Brandi?"

"I saw Shane. She's running around here snapping pictures."

"Cool, I'll find her a little bit later. You look nice."

"You're not looking so bad yourself, Marisa," he said, looking at her with a steady gaze.

"Well," she said, feeling a bit frazzled, "I should let you get back to—"

"Amanda."

"Right ... Amanda." Why was she feeling jealous? Matt was not her boyfriend. She cursed herself for feeling that way.

"Yeah, she's a cool girl, but she wasn't really my first choice for homecoming.

I couldn't go with the person I wanted 'cause ... well, let's just say it wouldn't have been right."

She suddenly became aware of her heartbeat. "Matthew—"

"I'll see you on Monday, Mari." Their eyes locked before he turned away. She watched him walk over to Amanda. She didn't realize that Ashley was watching her watch him. It was all Ashley needed.

CHAPTER 10

Brandi

As Brandi added the finishing touches to her makeup, she heard a knock at the door. She could hear her father talking to Brendon and felt utterly mortified that her two worlds were colliding. Her parents never seemed to mind when she was dating Matthew. They were both in middle school, and her parents knew the Kincades. They had questioned her relentlessly about Brendon. After all, he was an upperclassman who drove and stayed out later than the average freshman.

Brandi ran to Brendon's rescue just as her father was asking, "So, what time is this dance going to be over?"

Well, isn't this cute, she thought, *he's playing the caring-father role*. Brandi had mixed feelings ... on the one hand, she liked that her father was paying attention to her, but on the other, she was annoyed that he only did so at his own convenience. "Daddy," she chimed in as though they had the perfect *Leave It to Beaver* home. "I told you I would come straight home. Don't worry about me."

Brendon was looking at Brandi as if it was his first time seeing her. "You look amazing, Brandi," he said.

"Yes, she does." Her father interrupted Brendon's extra-long gaze at his daughter.

"I'll bring her straight home, sir."

"You'd better."

Just then her mother ran down the stairs with a camera to take their picture. "I am so sorry. I was on the phone," she said. They posed, she snapped it, and off they went to the dance.

In the car, Brendon was playing old-school slow jams that he had downloaded on his iPod. It was just what Brandi imagined their date would be like. The music and the twinkling night sky created a romantic ambience, which only heightened Brandi's anticipation. "So after we leave the dance, I have a surprise for you," his voice interrupted her thoughts.

"Well, you know the way to a girl's heart. I love surprises."

When they arrived at the dance, the first thing Brandi did was look for Shane and Marisa. She spotted Shane and noticed that she was moving a mile a minute. In the few seconds she watched her, she ran into a couple while taking another couple's picture, dropped her camera bag, and became really frustrated. Brandi ran over to help her pick up the contents of her bag. "You okay, Shane?"

she asked. Shane had been acting funny lately. Brandi couldn't put her finger on it, but something was different about her.

"Girl, I'm fine. You look so cute! Don't hurt him too much," she said, surveying Brandi's dress as it hugged the silhouette of her perfectly shaped body.

"Thanks! You're looking good too, darlin'."

The girls spotted Marisa and the other twirlers by the refreshment table and went over to her. "Mari!" they said as they all hugged.

"Girl, we're looking something fierce tonight!" Brandi exclaimed. "I love it when a plan comes together."

Marisa told the girls about the entrance she made with the other twirlers. "I can't wait to see what else Hayley has up her sleeve."

Brandi told them that Brendon had a surprise for her, and they were all excited in anticipation. "It's probably a ring or a necklace," she gushed. "Or maybe that teddy bear I spied at the mall."

"Girl, you never know what it is with Brendon. He's so classy. He may have a candy-painted limo waiting for you outside with champagne and caviar," Shane said. She sounded like she was writing a Danielle Steele novel.

"I am so happy that you're writing for the paper, Shane. Now you can cool it on the dramatics when we're having a regular conversation. What junior has champagne and caviar after homecoming?" Marisa asked.

"The kind I'm looking for," Shane said, dancing to the music that filled the cafeteria. "Anyway, I have to get back to work." *Snap, snap* ... she took pictures of the girls. "Y'all are the flyest broads here!" she exclaimed as she walked away.

They watched her walk, no ... run. "Wait, was that a skip?" Brandi asked. "Notice anything funny about Shane?"

"Yeah, but I don't know what," answered Marisa. "She's been acting strange since last night."

"No, it started before that. And it's just getting worse. We should ask her later." Just as they were about to part ways, Ashley and her crew came walking up to them. Both girls braced themselves for another endless confrontation.

"*Hola, chicas,*" Ashley said.

"What, Ashley?" Brandi snapped.

"*Nada.* I just saw you two together and was so impressed." Her voice dripped with sarcasm.

"Impressed?" Brandi said, rolling her eyes. She knew what was coming would not be a compliment.

"Yeah, I don't know if I would be speaking to my best friend if she was kissing all over my ex-boyfriend after he brought her home from Jerry's. You two are remarkable!" she said with a sly smirk. "Just remarkable."

"You're always tryna to start drama," Brandi cut her off before she could keep going.

"Oh, take it up with your precious little Marisa. Don't be mad if I have a go at Mattie next since he's community property. Y'all have fun at the dance," she drawled. Ashley and her friends left, laughing at Marisa and Brandi. They might not get a chance to see the drama, but they knew that they had started some, which made their night.

Brandi turned to Marisa and gave her a hug. She didn't want Ashley to think that her plan to make them angry with each other had succeeded. She whispered in her ear, "We'll talk about this later."

Brandi left Marisa standing alone as she walked over to Brendon and gave him a huge hug. She was determined not to let Matthew ruin her evening. Yes, she was hurt, but she couldn't allow it to affect her relationship with Brendon. She was already on thin ice after the stunt she pulled when she saw Marisa with Matthew at Jerry's. She decided she would talk to Marisa about it later. If it was true, she wasn't sure if she still wanted to be friends with her. If it wasn't true, then they would have to get back at that conniving little Ashley for trying to start trouble between them.

"So, you ready to leave?" Brendon asked.

"Leave? Brendon, we just got here. It's only eleven o'clock. I thought we were going to party until two in the morning. I know you aren't trying to head in early on me."

"Of course not. I told you that I had a surprise for you. Plus, nobody stays for the whole dance. That's only for freshmen. You're dating a junior ... you'll learn. We take pictures, then bounce. Anything else is just lame."

She thought he would give her the present at the dance so that she could show it off to her friends, but he obviously wanted to go somewhere private. Brendon was right. She was dating a junior, not some little freshman. *I guess it's time to learn how high schoolers party*, she thought. "Okay, but this had better be good," she warned him.

"Oh, it will be. Don't worry about that," he said, kissing her on the neck.

Brendon had the slow jams playing low in the car. Brandi was looking through his iPod for something to listen to when she felt the car slowing down and looked up to see where they were. They were turning into the Holiday Inn. "What are we doing at a hotel?" she asked, stunned.

"Girl, this is your surprise! One of my homies is throwing a party here tonight, and I knew you'd never been to a hotel party, so I thought it would be cool. It's chill, right?"

"Yeah, of course," she said, trying to sound cool with it, but she wasn't. The only time she had been in a hotel was when she was five and her family had gone to Disneyland. It made her remember when her family was happy. She always felt a little sad when she thought about her family now—more than she was willing to admit. She could either go to this party with Brendon or protest it and wind up at home listening to another endless fight between her mom and dad. She chose to stay.

When they got up to the room, Brendon's friends and their dates were there. They were drinking bottles of wine and cheap alcohol. "You want something to drink, babe? They have wine, Boones, or MD."

"Do they have Coke?"

"Girl, loosen up. I'll take care of you and get you home safely."

She smiled. "Okay, okay. I'll have some wine." He brought over a Styrofoam cup filled with some kind of pink liquid. "What is it?" she asked, smelling the cup.

"It's white zinfandel, just try it. You'll like it."

She took a sip. *Not so bad*, she thought. They found a spot on the bed where they could sit and talk comfortably, but it seemed that Brendon had more on his mind than talking. Brandi had kissed Brendon before, but this was different. They were in a hotel room, sitting on a bed, and something just seemed wrong. She thought that this was too much and too soon. It was different from what she had expected. She was wishing that Shane was right about the champagne and caviar. Anything would have been better than a hotel with a whole bunch of people getting drunk and making out. This was not her scene.

How did I get here? she thought to herself. *I just wanted to go to the dance and have fun with my friends. I wonder what Shane and Marisa are doing right now. Ugh, Marisa ... I don't even want to think about her. What time is it? I hope it's almost curfew. That'll be a good excuse to get out of here.* She pulled away from Brendon. "What time is it?" she asked.

He leaned back in to kiss her again.

"Brendon, stop. What time is it?"

He looked at his cell phone. "One fifteen."

"I'd better be getting home. Can we stop for something to eat?"

"Umm, okay," he responded, obviously upset by her abruptly ending their date. "Brandi, can I ask you something? Do you like me at all? It seems that I'm more for show to you. I'm trying to get to know you and you're pushing me away."

"I'm not pushing you away, Brendon, but this is all new for me."

"I get it, but if you're not ready for all of this, then I'm gonna have to find another girl who is." His attitude caught Brandi off guard. She did like Brendon, and being with him was a whole lot better than being alone. She had to figure out how to keep him interested. She had never dated anybody so experienced before. She would have to step up her game.

CHAPTER 11

Shane

When Shane separated from the girls at the dance, she began taking pictures of the other couples. She had popped her pill for the night, and it was helping her make it through the long evening. At about midnight, she started to feel a little faint and went to the restroom to splash water on her neck. She would have put it on her face if the girls at MAC hadn't made her look as clean as a new Gucci bag. As her hands ran under the stream of water, she noticed they were trembling so much that she could hardly hold the water. *What's going on?* she wondered.

She decided to go find Riley and tell her what was happening. She looked everywhere but couldn't find her, so she stepped outside to get some air.

As soon as she stepped outside, she heard somebody call her name from a parked car. Shane turned to see Riley sitting in her homie's car with a pipe in her hand. "Girl, what are you doing? You're smoking on school grounds! Are you insane, Riley?"

"Quit tripping," Riley responded in hushed tones. "Do you see anybody around here?"

Shane looked around. The parking lot was empty. "What'cha doing out here anyway?" asked Riley. Shane didn't want to tell Riley about her dizzy spell in front of her friend, so she told her she was just getting some air. "Why don't you get in?" Riley suggested.

Shane thought about it. When those pills were too strong, weed would usually even her out, so she reluctantly got into the car. *Maybe a little hit of weed will help*, she thought. "Hey," she said to the driver, who was obviously stoned out of his mind.

"Yooo ..." he responded. Even that one word was slurred.

Riley passed her the pipe. After the first puff, she began to calm down, and her hands didn't seem to be shaking as badly. She leaned against the backseat. It had been so long since her body was at rest. They passed it to her again, and she inhaled as hard as she could. *The more, the better*, she thought.

But that puff didn't calm her down or mellow her out. Instead, her heart started to beat uncontrollably. She didn't want to seem like she couldn't handle her weed, but the mix of the smoke and the pill in the stuffy car was doing something to her.

"Riley? Riley?" she thought she said. But Riley didn't hear her ...

When Shane opened her eyes again, Riley was sitting next to her in the backseat of the car. Her face felt wet, and she didn't know what was going on. "Riley," she said, beginning to panic. "What just happened?"

The kid from the driver's seat was just looking at her. "That almost blew my high," he said with a sigh.

Riley ignored him and responded to Shane, rubbing her arm. "Girl, I don't know! I was in the front seat listening to music, and I told you to come back to the dance with me, but you didn't respond. Then I jumped in the backseat and tried to shake you awake. I started screaming your name and you didn't say nothin'! It was so freaky! I wet a napkin and put in on your face. I guess the cool napkin worked 'cause here we are. Are you okay? Do you want to go to the hospital? Should I call your mom?"

"Nah, I'm good. It's no big deal. I think I'm just dehydrated because I was running around the dance like a maniac," Shane said with a nervous laugh.

"Okay, but you really need to slow down. Drink the rest of my water, and we'll get some more when we go inside."

Once inside, they were on their way over to the refreshment table to get more bottled water when they saw Mrs. Monroe walking toward them. Shane's hand instinctively reached for the camera that was supposed to be hanging around her neck.

"Hello there, girls. Let's go ahead and get your equipment turned in so that you can enjoy the rest of the dance."

Riley handed her camera over, but Shane didn't know where hers was. *Where was the last place I had it?* She panicked. *Oh no! It must be in that kid's car!* "Mrs. Monroe, I went out to talk to my mom earlier. I think I forgot it in the car," Shane lied.

"Shane, you were not supposed to take the camera out of the building."

"I know, Mrs. Monroe. I'm sorry. It was an accident. I'll call her right now." After Mrs. Monroe walked away, Shane turned to Riley, "I left the camera in your friend's car. Please call him. Do you think he would steal it?"

"Girl, I don't know him that well. We just smoke together. You'd better pray." Riley called, but she didn't get an answer. She tried texting him, but that didn't work either.

"What am I gonna do?" Shane was freaking out. "Mrs. Monroe is going to be furious. I can't deal with all of this right now."

"Calm down. It'll be okay."

"You don't know that, Riley. I could be in big trouble. I have to get that camera back. Okay, I need to get outta here before Mrs. Monroe sees me again. Hopefully I'll have it back before Monday."

CHAPTER 12

The Confrontation

Brandi, Marisa, and Shane dragged themselves out of bed the next morning. They all attended First Christian Church and sat together each Sunday morning. It had been a crazy weekend, and church was pretty much the last place the girls wanted to be.

Pastor Moore ended the sermon in a timely fashion, and the girls went over to Pappadeaux's to grab some lunch. "Well?" Brandi stated when the girls sat down.

"Well what?" Shane asked suspiciously.

"Not you, Shane. We'll get to you later. Marisa knows that I'm talking to her." Marisa didn't look up. She was playing with her bread and butter but never actually took a bite.

"What's going on here?" Shane asked.

"Oh, you didn't tell her, Marisa? Ashley said that she saw Marisa and Matt in the car together, and they were all hugged up and kissing."

"What?! Mari, that's not true ... is it?" Shane asked as Marisa began to cry. She never looked at Brandi or Shane. She just looked down.

"Say something!" Brandi yelled. People started to look at them, and Brandi tried to calm herself down.

"I'm sorry, B! I'm so, so sorry."

Brandi stormed off in tears. Shane had been completely blindsided; she had her own problems to deal with. The guy who had her camera hadn't called or anything, and now she had to be the shoulder for them to cry on. Where was *her* shoulder?

"Mari, I'm sorry, but … I have to check on B. This was really harsh." Shane got up and found Brandi crying in a bathroom stall. "Brandi, let me in."

"No! I don't want to talk about it, Shane. I can't wrap my head around all of this. She's … like my sister!" Brandi said through her sobs.

"Exactly, she *is* like your sister. Just come back out and talk to her."

"I don't want to talk to her. I don't know if I ever want to talk to her again!"

"Don't say that, B! Come on, get yourself together and we'll go back out there. I'll be here for you."

With that, Brandi opened the stall door, cleaned up her face, put on fresh makeup, and took a deep breath. "I'm only doing this for you, Shane," she said as she walked out of the restroom. When they returned to the table, Marisa was gone.

"I'm glad she's gone," spat Brandi. "I was gonna have to stop myself from slapping her across the face."

"Hey, this is Mari you're talking about."

"Yeah, that's why I'm so mad ... because it *is* Mari." Brandi was more hurt than anything. "She wasn't supposed to do this, Shane. She was supposed to be my best friend!" Tears started to pour from Brandi's eyes again.

"Sometimes people just make bad decisions, Brandi. We aren't perfect. I know you're mad right now, but maybe one day you'll be able to forgive her."

"It's too soon to even think about forgiving her. And of course Pastor's sermon would be on forgiveness today ... that was the last thing that I wanted to hear."

"It's also what you probably needed to hear the most," Shane said, laughing. "Well, I know that y'all are gonna work this out. I love you both too much to lose either of you."

"Shane, I can't stay friends with Marisa just because we've been friends for so long. I don't know. I just don't know." She paused and played with her fried shrimp. "I hate that it was Ashley who saw them."

"*You?* I know Marisa *really* hates it. Honey, I have to get going. I ... um ... have some business to take care of for the school newspaper."

"On a Sunday? That's crazy! Mrs. Monroe is working you too hard. How's it going anyway?"

"It's a lot of work, but I am up for it."

"Good for you. You're doing a great job. I'm so proud of you."

"Thanks, B. Sometimes I feel like I'm over my head, but if I can't get it done, then who can?"

"You know that's right!" The girls parted ways, each with a heavy heart.

What was supposed to be their traditional Sunday lunch—which was usually filled with fun and laughter—was heavy, awkward, and complicated. High school had changed them already. The honeymoon stage was over and real life was slapping them in the face.

CHAPTER 13

Brandi

When Brandi got home, all she wanted to do was talk to her mom. She would know what advice to give her when dealing with Marisa. But she could hear her parents' voices before she even reached the door. "Where's the money for the light bill, James?" her mom demanded.

"I had another bill to pay! I told you that!" her dad snapped.

"I don't care. I hid that money from you so that our children would have lights, and you took it! You have to be the most selfish, no good—

Crash. Brandi heard something break in the house.

She ran in and saw her mom threatening her dad. She had the broom clutched tightly in her hand, and it seemed like anger was dripping from her pores. One of her mom's favorite vases lay on the floor in pieces. "Mom, that's enough. Raven's gonna hear you ... please ..." Brandi already had enough to deal with, and she had to come home to this? What a miserable existence. She ran upstairs and found Raven sitting on her bed in tears.

"They've been arguing for an hour. Where *were* you?"

"I went out to lunch after church. I'm so sorry you were alone," said Brandi. "Let's get outta here. You wanna go out for some ice cream?" Raven nodded her head. They headed to the Marble Slab down the street.

"Brandi, do you think Mom and Dad are gonna get a divorce?" Raven asked as she ate her banana nut ice cream.

"I don't know, Raven. They have a lot of issues to work out. I don't even know if it's healthy for them to stay together at this point. I think that Dad's really sick."

"Is he going to die?" she asked, concern clouding her face.

"No ... not that kind of sick." Brandi didn't want to say what was really going on with her father. She had figured it out on her own many years ago, but Raven was too young to know the truth. Nobody wanted to hear that their father was a drug addict. No eight-year-old should have to. "Don't worry about Dad. He'll be better one day," Brandi said as she hugged her sister. She just hoped that it was true.

Lately, it had been Brandi's job to make sure that Raven was being taken care of. The more stress her mother was under to pay the bills and keep their finances in order, the more responsibilities Brandi had to take on. Why couldn't she be like her friends? Their main concern was school and fun. Hers was not. To the outside world, she had a perfect life. She was smart, pretty, and funny. She dated one of the hottest guys in the school. She was a cheerleader for goodness' sake. Most other girls envied her. *How ironic!* she thought.

Usually she was able to keep up appearances, but right now it was hard. She was feeling so low. First there was the Marisa and Matthew thing, and now her parents' fighting. Who could she turn to? She felt so alone. She wasn't ready to shatter the perfect image that Brendon had of her, so she just avoided him. It was difficult to hide the sadness in her voice. He kept dialing her number, but she didn't answer the phone. On call number five, she decided to pick up.

"Hello?"

"Are you avoiding me?"

"Um ... no," she lied. "Why would you think that?"

"I don't know. I was a jerk Friday night. I just wanted to apologize."

"You're right. You were a butt, and I accept your apology."

"So ... you busy? You wanna hang out and catch a movie or something?"

"Well, I have my little sister with me. We're at Marble Slab, but we're heading home."

"I have a better idea. I'll pick you two up, we'll catch a movie, and then I'll bring you home. Cool?"

"Cool!" Brandi was feeling better already. She was so happy that she was dating Brendon. Their relationship was the one aspect of her life where she could find some peace. That was one of the reasons why she was so disappointed when he snapped at her after the dance. Of course, she understood that the other girls Brendon had dated were older than her and had probably been to numerous parties like the one he took her to. But drinking, partying, making out? She just wasn't comfortable with that scene. Didn't he realize that she was an inexperienced freshman new to the high school dating scene?

Brendon pulled into the parking lot to pick them up. "Get in, gorgeous!" he yelled. Brandi and Raven both jumped in the car. They headed to the theater. Brendon bought their tickets, snacks, and drinks. He was spoiling her. He knew he had been wrong on Friday, and spoiling her was his way of making it right. This was a much better surprise than any stupid hotel party.

Shoot, I could get used to this, she thought. What she didn't think about was all that he would want in return.

CHAPTER 14

Marisa

After Marisa left Pappadeaux's, she didn't know where to go. She wasn't in the mood to go home, and she couldn't be around her own friends. She decided it was going to be a quiet afternoon of watching Telemundo and eating popcorn. She just wanted to hide.

"*Bueno, bebé*," her mom said, kissing her on the cheek as she smoothed her hair.

"Hey, Mama," she replied and went to her room without saying another word. She didn't want to talk to her mom about what happened. Nobody would understand. While she lay on the bed watching the *novellas* she had taped during the week, her phone rang. It was Matt. She thought about switching his caller ID to read "too complicated," but it was too long to spell out. Reluctantly she answered. "Hello?"

"Hey, Mari! What'cha doing?" Matthew always seemed oblivious to the drama that he caused between the girls, so much so that Marisa never wanted to bring it up, so she didn't.

"Nothing, what's up?"

"Um … I was wondering if you wanted to take a ride with me. I think we really need to talk."

"Matt, I don't think that's such a good idea." She was not in the mood for more drama with Brandi. It wasn't like she wanted to fight with her. Brandi was her bestie, after all.

"Look, Marisa, I wanna talk to you, but I wanna do it face-to-face. I promise it won't take long. And I'll be on my best behavior."

That statement made Marisa laugh, and she gave in. "Okay, but I can't be out long."

Matthew arrived at Marisa's house feeling slightly nervous. He knew how he felt, but he didn't know how to tell Marisa. He would have to feel it out.

Marisa brought out a plate of *sopapillas* that her mother had just finished making and two lime *Jaritos*. They talked for a while, but there was no way to ignore the elephant in the room. What were they *doing*? "So why are you here, Matthew?" she asked, looking him squarely in the eye.

"Um ... well ..." Matthew was obviously nervous and searching for his words. He played with one of the sopapillas that she served, but he had yet to take a bite. "Okay, Mari, I don't know how else to put this ..." He looked her directly in the eyes and said,

"I have feelings for you. I just do. I didn't mean to, and I don't wanna hurt Brandi even more than I already have, but ... I feel like you have feelings for me too. I just want to see where this can take us."

"Stop! I can't do this, Mattie. I just can't. What you're saying to me ... it's just not right. Do you realize that Brandi's already not talking to me? Do you realize that I could lose my best friend? Do you realize that you cheated on her this summer, and you would probably do the same thing to me? Do you realize—"

"Yes, Marisa. I realize all of that. You don't have to keep going. This was a mistake. I should go ..." he said, standing up abruptly.

"Yeah, maybe you should," she said. With that, Matthew walked out of Marisa's house. He sat in his car with his feelings hurt and looked back toward the house. She was looking out the window, and their eyes met one last time. Marisa quickly shut the curtains and went to her room. She cried into her pillow for what seemed like hours. She felt like she had lost two good friends, and all she had the energy to do was cry.

CHAPTER 15

Shane

Lunch was not what Shane had expected it to be. She had gone out to eat with her friends to forget about the drama brewing in her life, but she ended up walking into even more of it. She was lost as to how Marisa could hurt Brandi like that. She didn't even know what to say to her. However, she had to get her mind off of them and on to the fact that she still had not located her school camera.

As soon as she left the restaurant, she called Riley. "Have you heard anything from your boy yet?" she asked hopefully.

"Girl, no. I called everybody who knows him. There's still hope, Shane."

"I should've never gotten into that car, Riley. I should've never—"

"Shane, we'll fix this. Let me go. I have a few more people I can reach out to."

Shane sat there reeling. She didn't know what she was going to do if she couldn't locate that camera. What would Mrs. Monroe think? Would her parents be responsible for replacing it? What would she tell them? Not the truth, she thought. How would it sound? "Mom, Dad, I lost the camera because I was hopped up on pills and needed to smoke some weed to level out. Then I passed out in the car and with all the excitement, I forgot the camera on some guy's seat. ... Who is he? Um ... I don't know ... he's just the weed man." No, the truth would definitely not work. She had to come up with something else.

As Shane walked into the kitchen where her mother was cooking, she braced herself. She was about to lie to her mother. It was something she was never really good at doing. But she had no choice this time; she was the only one who could help her out of this situation. She didn't want her to hear about the camera from some-one at the school. She needed her mom to be on her side. "Mom," she said.

"Yeah, baby? What do you need?" her mom responded but never took her eyes off the stove where the pot roast, mashed potatoes, macaroni and cheese, and Glory green beans were culminat-ing into another perfect Sunday dinner. Shane would normally be excited at the thought of a delicious dinner with her family. But she was so sick with worry about the camera that this meal was actually making her feel queasy.

"I need to talk to you about something that happened on Friday."

Her mom pulled an apple cobbler out of the oven and looked her daughter squarely in the eye. "What, baby? What happened?" she asked, looking worried.

"Well ..." she could feel her phone vibrate in her pocket and glanced at it. It was Riley. "Mom, I have to take this. Give me a sec."

"Girl, I found him!" Riley shouted. "He said that he is on his way over here. He was passed out at his cousin's house."

"Oh, Riley! I can't believe it! Saved again! I'll be there in ten." She didn't even notice that her mother was standing right behind her with a worried look on her face. "Mom, I gotta go. I'll talk to you when I get back."

"Shane," her mother said in an accusing tone, "what's going on? You know that I don't like you hanging out with Riley."

"It's nothing, Mom. Everything is fine now. Just fine."

Shane got to Riley's house just as the dude pulled up with the camera. Riley was talking to him through the window. "Now, you know I didn't think you did my girl wrong, Mario. We were just worried that we wouldn't be able to reach you before Monday. Thank you so much for bringing the camera!"

"You have no idea how you saved my butt, Mario," Shane smiled. "Thanks again."

Riley asked, "You wanna come out back? I've already got it rolled up." Shane knew instantly that she should go home. This camera situation was a close call, and she didn't want to get into any more trouble.

Mario followed Riley to the backyard, but Shane didn't move.

"Riley, I've had enough drama, and I don't need any more. I'll see you tomorrow."

"You can come out back and chill with us. We're here because of you. This is your celebratory blunt!" She laughed.

"Fine, but leave me out of the rotation."

Riley and Mario smoked while Shane kept them company. She wasn't sure when or how it happened that it was passed to her, but she didn't refuse it when it was. Once again, Shane had succumbed to the weed. It wasn't peer pressure that was hurting Shane ... it was Shane herself. She took the ten-minute walk home and realized that she was about to walk into her house extremely high.

"Shane," she heard her mom call from the living room. "Your father and I want to talk to you."

Shane dragged herself into the room.

"So, what's going on? What happened on Friday? Why did you run out of here like that, and why were you with Riley? You know I don't like—wait a minute." Her mother stopped talking and looked at her suspiciously. "Shane, are you high?"

Shane felt totally panicked. Her eyes were red and she reeked of weed. "No," she lied. She could see in her parents' eyes that they didn't believe her.

"Shane, go to your room," her father said. "I can't even look at you right now. You are obviously high and obviously lying, but don't worry about it. I have something for you," he hinted.

Shane panicked. She had been stressed out all weekend. The last thing she needed were her parents on her back. "What? You're going to ground me? You know what, Dad? You need to worry about you and stop worrying about me and my business. Since when did you two decide to play parents anyway?" She knew that she was out of line, but she couldn't stop herself. All of her emotions surfaced at that moment and she wanted to lash out.

"Shane, that is enough! Go to your room before we all say or do something that we can't take back," her mother shouted.

Shane ran up the stairs and bumped into Robin. "What was that?" Robin asked.

"Why are you giving Mom and Dad a hard time? Are you high again? I thought that was behind you. I thought you were turning your life around this year."

"Bite me, Robin! I'm sorry I can't be as perfect as you. I'm just me, good old-fashioned me, and I'm not apologizing for it. So you can kick rocks!" With that, Shane walked away and slammed her bedroom door as hard as she could. She fell onto her pillow and sobbed. *What just happened?* she thought to herself. She didn't mean it ... she really didn't.

CHAPTER 16

Intervention

Monday morning arrived and all three girls were reluctant to go to school. Shane's mind was on her family's fighting and her meeting with Mrs. Monroe. Brandi was deep in thought about her own family and her relationship with Brendon. Marisa couldn't stop thinking about how uncomfortable her classes with Matthew would be, and she dreaded seeing Brandi. They thought junior high was difficult, but it was nothing compared to the problems they were having since they started high school. For the first time, they each felt alone. They couldn't even turn to each other.

At 8:05 in the morning, the girls ran into each other at their lockers. Avoidance was not an option; they had structured their lives to see each other as much as possible. "Hey," Shane said to the girls as they all started rummaging through their lockers in preparation for the day. "I was wondering if we could go to Jerry's today and talk. Yesterday didn't end so hot, and this is the last week before Thanksgiving break. I'll miss y'all too much if we don't straighten this thing out."

"I have practice," Brandi said dryly.

"Okay, after practice, then."

"I'm really not in the mood, Shane," but she stared at Marisa when she said it.

"Please, Brandi? We *do* need to talk," Marisa said, looking like a lost puppy.

"Look, I don't want to talk to you, Mari. I just don't," Brandi said with tears welling up in her eyes.

At that moment, Marisa didn't care if Brandi was mad at her. She reached out, grabbed her, and hugged her as tightly as she could. "Please, B," she whispered in her ear. Brandi pulled away from her and nodded, wiping her tears away.

"Now that's what I'm talking about. Show some love to your girl too," Shane said jokingly. The girls laughed and parted ways. Each of them was deep in thought, trying to figure out how to overcome the new obstacles that seemed to be coming at them a mile a minute.

They all arrived at Jerry's at different times. Marisa and Brandi both arrived before Shane, and any onlooker could tell they were not comfortable. There was an awkward silence between the girls while they chose which words to say to each other. After a minute, they both began to talk at the same time. "Go ahead," Marisa said.

"No, Mari. I really wanna hear what you have to say."

Marisa sighed. She had this conversation all planned out in her head: *I'm sorry. It'll never happen again. We had a moment of weakness when we were both vulnerable.* For some reason she didn't say that, though. Instead, she heard herself saying, "I think I'm really falling for him, B. I never meant for this to happen." Tears streamed down her face.

"What am I supposed to say to that, Mari? We just broke up five months ago. I made peace with having to see him with someone else, but I never thought it would be *you*. It hurts in a different way."

"You know how much I love you, B?" They were both crying at this point.

"Yeah, Mari ... I know."

"Well then, you know I didn't want to hurt you. Something happened between us that we didn't expect. I didn't even see it coming. We spend every school day together. We have five classes together, and we're lab partners. Dang ... I just didn't see it coming."

"So, where are we supposed to go from here? What do you want from me?" Brandi asked.

"I want ... no, I *need* your blessing, *mi amore*. If I don't get it, then he's history. You're more important to me than anybody ... you and Shane."

Brandi stared into Marisa's eyes. "Go for it, Mari. Do it! I obviously couldn't make Matthew happy, but I don't want to keep you from your happiness."

Marisa jumped up from her side of the booth and hugged Brandi. "You are too good to me. I love you."

"I love you too. Look, Shane's coming now." They watched Shane and then looked at each other. Shane seemed odd again. They both knew something was wrong with her, but they couldn't figure out what.

"I'm here! Did I miss anything?" she asked as she started fishing through her purse looking for something. She dumped out all of its contents on the table. "I can't find my wallet," she said.

"Shane, slow down. It's right there," Marisa said, pointing to it.

"Wow, how did I not see that? I'm trippin'."

"Ya think?" Brandi asked sarcastically.

Shane rolled her eyes. "So what's up? You two look like you've made up. Was it a case of mistaken identity or what?"

"No, not exactly. We decided we're just gonna part ways. It's too awkward now that Marisa and Mattie have decided to date."

"What?! Who made *that* decision?" Marisa and Brandi started laughing at Shane's reaction. She narrowed her eyes and shook her head, "Ah, you got me," she said.

"No, really, Shane. Marisa likes Mattie, and I just gave her my blessing for them to move forward."

"*What?*" Shane's reaction wasn't much different than it had been the first time. "Who made that decision?" she repeated. They laughed again. The truth sounded just as ludicrous as the made-up story, but the girls would do anything to save their relationships with one another.

"So, Shane, what's been going on with you?" Brandi asked, changing the subject.

"What do you mean? Nothing ..." Shane responded defensively. Brandi and Marisa glanced at each other, and Shane didn't miss their exchange. "What are you two trippin' about? Now that you aren't mad anymore, you're ganging up on me? That's perfect," she said, annoyed with the girls for butting into her life.

"Shane, you're not gonna do this again. Stop looking for reasons to get mad at us.

You know you can tell us anything, right? I know your life has totally changed this year. That must be difficult for you. You don't always have to be so strong. You can lean on us if you need to," Brandi said, pouring her heart out to her best friend.

"Brandi, you're the stupidest smart person I know. You should be more concerned with Marisa's hand in your cookie jar instead of all up in my business. And, Marisa, you're such a slut. You're happy with your best friend's sloppy seconds. Seriously, you two are pathetic!" And with that, Shane stormed off.

"O-kay, that didn't go well. We have to figure out what's going on with Shane," Marisa pointed out. "That wasn't the Shane we know. She's using her anger to cover something up, but what can it be? What's so bad that she won't tell us?"

"Maybe we should talk to Riley about it. Do you think she's been talking to her?"

"Shane would be livid if we went to

Riley, and you know Riley can't hold water. She would tell her."

"You know what? Shane is just gonna have to be mad, then, because I'm gonna do whatever it takes to get to the bottom of this. Shane wouldn't stop until she saved both of us. Now it's our turn to save her.

"Something's wrong, Mari," Brandi continued. "How else are we gonna find out what it is? When Shane was going through all of her drama last year, she pulled away from us. That made the situation much worse, and now she's doing it again."

"I know, B. So what's the plan?"

"Well, first we have to think like Shane. What would she do in this situation?"

"The question is," Mari added, "what *wouldn't* she do if we were in trouble?"

The girls put their heads together to come up with a foolproof plan that would shed some light on what their friend was going through. They weren't going to let her down. It was too important.

CHAPTER 17

Shane

$\mathcal{I}$t was finally Thanksgiving break, and nobody needed it like Shane Foster. She was exhausted. She had met all of her deadlines before the break. When she turned everything in, Mrs. Monroe gave her great feedback for a job well done. "I am so proud of you, Shane. When I had you head up the freshmen section of the yearbook, I knew you'd do a good job, but you have done better than I could have imagined."

"Thanks, Mrs. Monroe," she said, smiling.

"Are you all right, Shane? You look down for some reason."

"I'm fine, Mrs. Monroe. I just have a lot of work to do for my classes. Have a happy Thanksgiving."

"Same to you, Shane," Mrs. Monroe responded.

She took Mrs. Monroe's compliments with a smile on her face and a frown in her heart. Mrs. Monroe had no idea what Shane was doing to get the job done. Nobody did. She didn't even tell Riley about the effects the pills were having on her body. After that first time Shane blacked out, the blackouts just kept happening. She pretended that it didn't bother her. She told herself every day that this pill would be the last, but she couldn't stop. She knew it was bad, but she also knew that she needed the pills to get stuff done. It wasn't just the yearbook; she had seven classes and the teachers didn't seem to care when they piled on the work.

Shane wished she could confide in her friends, but everybody was so proud of her for turning her life around that she didn't want to disappoint them. She thought that she could stop taking the pills and smoking weed before anybody would even know about it. She had to; she didn't have a choice. This was not the high school high that she wanted.

Shane was so ashamed of how she had been treating her friends and her family. She was lying in bed with tears streaming down her face as she thought about the fights she had caused. She heard her cell vibrating and didn't want to move to answer it until she heard *All the single ladies*. She dove for the phone. "Hey, Mari," she said somberly.

"Hey, chica. You want some company today?"

"Are you sure you wanna hang out with me? I was such a butt to you and B."

"Of course I want to hang out with you. We all have our moments. I forgave you before you even thought about asking for forgiveness."

"I didn't ask for forgiveness, Mari."

"I know ... that's what I mean," she said with a laugh.

"I'm so sorry, Mari," she said with tears welling up in her eyes again. "I promise things are gonna change. I know I've been pretty weird lately, but I've just had a lot on my plate."

"Girl, it's all good. I can't wait to see you."

Shane hung up the phone and headed into the bathroom, excited that Marisa was coming over. She looked at herself in the mirror and instantly saw fatigue. She saw the dark circles under her eyes and decided that going without makeup was not an option. She opened the medicine cabinet and was just about to pop a pill. She stopped cold. She didn't have a deadline to meet or any other demands on her today, but she still had the urge. *What's happening to me?* she wondered.

She opened the pill bottle and there were only two left. That wouldn't even get her through Thanksgiving! She hurriedly grabbed the phone and called Riley. "Hey, Riley."

"Hey, Shane. What'cha doing? Enjoying your break?"

"Girl, yes," she said, trying to sound upbeat. "I've just been lying around being lazy. Hey, Marisa just called to come over, and I didn't want to drag around. I went to pop one of those energy pills and realized I don't have any left."

There was silence on the other end. "Hello?"

"Yeah, I'm here. Did you take *all* those pills already? I gave you a lot of pills. Are you giving them away or something?"

"Of course. You know I didn't take all of them myself," she lied.

"Girl, you had me nervous for a second. We don't need you passing out again like you did the night of the homecoming dance."

"I know," Shane said. "That was pretty scary."

"Well, you have, like, ten minutes to get over here because my mom and I are gonna catch a movie and it starts in twenty."

"I'll be there in five!" Shane glanced in the mirror and realized that she looked a hot mess, but she didn't have time to do any of the things she had planned—like brush her teeth, wash her face, comb her hair, or get dressed—there was no time. With her hair still wrapped and her pj's on, Shane arrived at Riley's house.

"Why do you look like that?" Riley asked in a whisper.

"Girl, you know I'm cute," Shane said, laughing.

"I know you didn't come walking down the street like that. That ain't even like you."

"You told me to hurry. Quit trippin'!" Shane was becoming increasingly uncomfortable with her appearance.

"Whatever, Shane," Riley said, obviously annoyed. "All I know is that I'm not gonna to be the reason for your demise. Don't ask me for any more pills."

"Okay, Riley. I see how it is."

"Look, I wouldn't have said yes to you this time if I knew you were looking cracked out."

"Cracked out? Riley Nichols, you have some nerve!" She was upset, but not upset enough to walk away without either the pills or something to smoke.

"I'm sorry, but you caught me off guard today. Take your package before my mom comes out. Just bounce 'cause she'll be all over me."

"Wow, so you're ashamed of me now? You don't want your family to see me?" Tears began to well up in Shane's eyes again. She was so embarrassed. "Hey ... do you have some weed too?"

Riley rolled her eyes and said, "Yeah, it's in there. I guess you'll tighten my purse strap later, huh?"

"You know I will! Thanks and have a happy Thanksgiving!"

"Yeah, you too," Riley said, looking worried about her friend. She instantly regretted hooking Shane up with the pills and the weed.

As Shane rounded the corner to her house, she could see someone sitting on the porch. "Shoot! I forgot all about Marisa!" she said to herself.

CHAPTER 18

Marisa

Marisa sat on Shane's porch waiting for her to answer the door. She had called and told her she was coming. Now she tried calling and texting her phone again, but she didn't get a response. *What in the world is going on with Shane?* she wondered.

There was so much going on in Marisa's world. She was trying to get to the bottom of what was happening with Shane, and that was totally stressing her out. She also really wanted to talk to Matt about moving forward with their relationship now that she had Brandi's blessing, but that would have to wait. Until this thing with Shane reached some sort of resolution, her feelings for Matt had to be put on the back burner. Shane was her main concern right now.

Just as she was about to give up, she saw someone coming down the street. It looked like it might be Shane, but that girl was looking raggedy. *Is that? No ... Shane would never be caught dead at noon walking around in her pj's ...* All of this ran through Marisa's head, but as the person got closer, she realized that it was Shane after all. "Why you look like that?" she asked abruptly.

Shane rolled her eyes as she approached the door. "Good morning to you too, Mari," she said snidely. "I hope you didn't come over here to give me crap."

"No ... but it's not morning any more. And I've been waiting for you for a while. You totally dissed me, and then you show up looking like ... like ... girl, I don't even know what you look like." Marisa could see that Shane was getting annoyed, and that was not part of the plan. She tried to make light of the situation so she could get into the house. "Anyway, let's just go chill out. I'm not tripping. It's Thanksgiving break, and I have nothing to do."

Shane unlocked the door, and they went upstairs to play some music. "So, what's the plan? Did you wanna do something today or just hang out?"

"I would love to swing by the mall for a little while. I need to get some gray boots to wear for Thanksgiving Day," Marisa said. "Not trying to clown or anything, but you are gonna change out of your pj's if we go somewhere ... right?"

Shane threw a pillow at Marisa playfully.

Marisa laughed and said, "Now scoot. Go get fly."

Shane retreated to the bathroom, and Marisa instantly grabbed Shane's purse to look through everything in it. She even looked at her call history. The last person she talked to was Riley. "I knew that she had something to do with this," she said aloud. Part one of the mission had been accomplished. One piece of the puzzle was fitting into place.

Shane came out of the bathroom with her hair laid and her makeup flawless. "Better?" she asked.

"You know it. I have to use the bathroom now. I worked up a full bladder waiting on your porch." Marisa retreated into the bathroom and started digging through the medicine cabinet and drawers. There was nothing of interest in the drawers, but there were some unidentified pills in the cabinet. *What could this be for?* she wondered. She took a picture of the pill and sent it over to Brandi so that she could investigate further.

"You okay in there?" Shane asked, knocking on the door.

"Yeah, I'm good. Just need a couple of seconds," she yelled, giving the toilet a flush. She ran the water in the sink to buy herself more time. She couldn't find anything else that looked askew. "This will have to do," she said mindlessly.

"Who are you talking to in there?" Shane asked, laughing.

"Like you don't talk to yourself," Marisa said as she walked back out. "Okay, let's get out of here. It's our break and we need to have some fun. Is Robin gonna bring us to the mall?"

"Let me check on her," said Shane. She knocked on Robin's door, but there was no answer. She called her phone and could hear it ringing inside her room. "Answer the door, woman. I know you're in there!" she shouted.

Robin came to the door looking like a train wreck. "What, li'l girl?" she asked, obviously annoyed and tired.

"Dang! What have you been doing?"

"Sleeping ... it's break. I was doing what normal seniors do this time of year. Only noisy li'l freshmen are bouncing around. What do you want, Shane?"

"Yo, bring me and Mari to the mall."

"Pay me and I'll take you. Five bucks for gas and a dollar for incidentals."

"Incidentals?"

"Yeah ... air, music, you name it. You two are paying for it."

"Girl, we can call a taxi for that."

"A'ight, peace."

"Robin! Quit tripping," Marisa chimed in. "You two are ridiculous."

They all laughed, and Robin shut the door to get dressed. As soon as she finished, they headed to the mall.

While they were shopping, Marisa was looking for an opportunity to get a moment alone with Robin. Finally she cornered Robin in the food court. "Look, I have to talk to you about something."

"All this food is making me sick to my stomach," Robin mumbled.

"Robin, focus! I only have a second to get this out before your sister comes back. Have you noticed anything different about her lately?"

"Yeah, she's been a butt to me and to our parents, but we all have bad days."

"No ... it's been going on for too long now. She's not just being a butt. Please don't tell Shane what I am about to tell you. You can't mention anything until we know more."

"Okay, you're scaring me. What is it?"

"I found a bottle of pills in Shane's medicine cabinet. I took a picture of one of them and sent it over to Brandi."

Robin didn't know whether she should be supporting Mari or slapping her for going through her sister's stuff. "So, you basically went digging through her things? I don't even do that, and I'm her sister. What the—"

Marisa cut her off. "Well, maybe you should have. I think Shane might be taking pills that aren't prescribed to her. Here she comes. I need your help if we're going to help Shane."

Robin tried to warn her as quickly as possible. "Mari, you know how Shane is. You'd better be sure about this because she will look at it like the highest form of betrayal if you aren't."

"What are you two over here yapping about?" Shane asked when she returned to the table. "Y'all are looking all serious."

"We're trying to figure out if we should go to Aldo or Forever 21. Do you get the shoes first or the outfit first? What do you think?"

"Is that a real question? Do you even know me? Shoes! We can swing by Aldo and Nine West. I think they're having a sale too."

They knew they had dodged a bullet with that one. Mari could hear her phone ringing. *All the single ladies, All the single ladies* ... She knew it was Brandi giving her the 411 on the pills. At first she hesitated. But she couldn't explain to Shane why she would be ignoring it, especially since they always picked up each other's calls. So she answered the phone and talked quickly. "What's up, B? I'm at the mall with Shane and Robin. What are you doing?"

"Girl, I'm surfing the net. Can you come by when you leave the mall? And, Mari, come alone. We need to talk." With that, Mari knew that she would need to find an excuse to get over to Brandi's without Shane tagging along.

While they were in Aldo, Mari was able to get Robin alone again. "Robin, I have to roll out. Brandi wants to see me and it's not sounding good."

"You two have me worried. Well, you can't just leave. What is Shane gonna think?" They both looked at Shane as she admired a pair of shoes in the mirror. Her leg was significantly thinner than it had been when school started.

Wow, she's so skinny," her sister said.

"That's what I've been trying to tell you, Robin. Something's wrong; this isn't our Shane. She's almost worse than last year. I'm gonna need your help getting out of here. Just tell her that I'm in the restroom. It'll only take a few minutes to get to Brandi's house."

"You want me to take you?"

"No, I don't want to tip Shane off. I'll make it over there. If she asks, I'm in the restroom and that's all you know."

"Got it. Hey, don't forget to call me. I want to know what's going on with my little sister too."

CHAPTER 19

Brandi

Brandi sat staring at her computer screen in disbelief. Shane was quite possibly the smartest person that Brandi had ever met, yet she could make some of the stupidest decisions. *My girl just thinks she's invincible*, Brandi thought to herself.

"Adderall?" she said aloud as if Shane could hear her. Just as she was trying to find out more information about the pills, she heard the doorbell ring. She ran to answer the door for Marisa. "Broad, hurry up and get in here."

"What did you find?"

"Shane's been taking Adderall."

"What's that? The ADHD medicine?" Marisa asked, confused.

"Exactly, but it's a deadly drug whether it's prescribed or not."

"Deadly? Don't be dramatic, B. A lot of people take it. It can't be that bad."

"I'm not being dramatic. Come read for yourself."

Marisa couldn't believe her eyes. It was so obvious that Shane was addicted to Adderall once they began researching it. She was irritable, moody, thin, and aggressive, and there was no telling what other symptoms she was experiencing that she wasn't telling them about. "Oh, B, this is more serious than I thought. I wanna confront Riley. I know this is her doing. Where else would Shane get Adderall?"

"I don't know, but what worries me the most is the fact that it can cause seizures, heart attacks, and even sudden death. I wonder if Shane knows about this. Did she research anything before she started popping pills?"

"Well, now that we know, what do we do next? Robin told me to holler at her when we knew some facts. I think they may still be at the mall, though."

"Where does she think you are?"

"She thinks I'm in the restroom." They both laughed, but their hearts were heavy with the reality of Shane's addiction.

"We could have an intervention," Brandi suggested.

"Um ... I don't think Shane's the inter-vention type."

"Yeah, well, we didn't think that she was the I'ma-turn-into-a-pillhead type either, but here we are."

"We need to talk to Robin. She'll know what to do."

"Okay, then you talk to Robin; I'm gonna talk to Riley." Shane was going to hate them for prying into her business, but someday she would get over it. They would rather her be alive and mad than the alternative.

Brandi walked over to Riley's house and waited for her on the porch. It was no secret that Brandi and Riley weren't the best of friends and for obvious reasons. Brandi felt that Riley was the reason Shane got into trouble in junior high. She always encouraged Shane to do the wrong things, and she never looked out for her well-being. Granted, Shane was a big girl with her own mind—which was always Riley's stance—but the things they did together just didn't gel with the Shane that Brandi and Marisa knew. "Hi, Ms. Nichols," Brandi said as Riley and her mother walked up the steps to their home.

"Hi, baby," replied Ms. Nichols. "How is your mother?"

"Oh, she's fine."

"Well, tell Cat I said hello. And you don't be such a stranger. I never see you around here anymore."

"I won't, Ms. Nichols," she lied, and Ms. Nichols went into the house.

"To what do I owe the honor?" Riley asked sarcastically.

Brandi rolled her eyes. "Not today, Riley, okay? I'm here because of Shane. Have you two been hanging out lately? I know that you're both on the yearbook committee."

"Of course we hang out. We're friends, Brandi. I know how much you hate that fact, but we are. So get over yourself."

Brandi felt her blood boiling, but she had to stay focused. This wasn't about her relationship with Riley. She just needed information, so she ignored Riley's comments. "Look, Riley, I didn't come over here to argue with you. I need your help."

"You need my help? Oh, this should be good."

"Well, Mari and I have noticed some weird stuff going on with Shane. She's been crazy lately. She goes off in a second for the smallest things. She's been really irritable, and she's losing a lot of weight. Have you noticed anything strange?"

"No, Brandi, and I'm not your little snitch. If you have a problem with Shane, then you need to take it up with her."

"You know what, Riley? You're probably the worst friend that Shane has ever had."

"The worst friend?"

"Yeah, all you do is think about yourself. It's all good when y'all are joyriding or smoking weed, but when she's in trouble, all you do is bail on her."

"I'm not bailing on her. Riley Nichols ain't nobody's snitch!"

"So, you do know about the Adderall, then?" Brandi said, as if she knew everything that had been going on.

"Yeah, I know about the Adderall. It's just ADHD medicine. You make it sound like she's smoking crack. You've always been whack, Brandi. Everybody's not stressing over who has the highest pyramid," she said mockingly.

"No, Riley, what I'm focused on is the fact that my friend is addicted to Adderall, and it's just as bad as crack! It can cause seizures and blackouts and it can even kill you. So there! If you're not worried, I am!" she screamed with tears rolling down her face.

Riley stood there, stunned. She had no clue that Adderall was so bad. How could she be so stupid? She never even thought that the pills were responsible for Shane blacking out in that car on homecoming night. And she was mixing it with weed. What had she done? She was the one who introduced her to Adderall. She softened toward Brandi. "Okay, Brandi, I have to tell you something. You can't tell Shane that

I'm telling you this. Homecoming night ... Shane passed out in my friend's car. She didn't come around for about two minutes. It felt like forever. I didn't know why. She said she was just dehydrated."

Brandi walked away from Riley, but Riley was right behind her. "Where are you going?"

"I'm going to find Shane," Brandi shouted.

"Well, I'm coming with you."

Brandi called Marisa. "Have you talked to Robin yet? ... Okay, you two stay put. I have Riley. We're on our way there."

"Where are we going?" Riley asked.

"Robin and Marisa are at Marisa's house. We have to hurry."

When they arrived, Robin was in Marisa's room, crying. "What's wrong now?"

"Girl, Shane and I fell out after Marisa left the mall. She said that we were being sneaky, and she would figure us out. She said a bunch of mean stuff to me and hopped on the bus. She's not at home, and she won't answer her cell phone. I don't know what's going on with my sister. You were right. She's worse than last year." Robin stopped as if she just realized that there was an intruder in their midst. "What's *she* doing here?" she asked, eyeing Riley suspiciously.

"I'm here for Shane, so lay off."

At that moment, Robin jumped up and got right in her face. "Don't let me find out that you had anything to do with this, Riley! So help me, I'll be on you like white on rice."

"Chill, Robin!" Brandi yelled. "We're all on the same team. We need to find Shane. We need to find out where she's getting these pills from and if she knows how dangerous they are."

Now it was Riley's turn to cry. "I gave her the p—"

Robin slapped Riley across her face before the word *pill* could escape her lips. "Misery loves company. You are such a loser, Riley. You're trying to bring Shane down. She's not like you, so stop trying to turn her into the trash you turned out to be," she screamed in her face.

Riley was usually ready for a good fight, but today she couldn't even retaliate. She knew that what she had done was wrong. "I didn't mean for this to happen. She's the one who started taking the pills every day, and she's the one blacking out. I didn't know these pills could do all of this. The guy I got them from didn't tell me either. I just knew that I had more energy. I swear ... I didn't want to hurt Shane." She was crying uncontrollably.

"Blacking out?" Robin screamed. "We have to find my sister," she said, collapsing on the bed in tears.

Marisa put her arm around Riley's shoulder. "I'm sure that you didn't mean to hurt Shane. She's a big girl who makes her own decisions, but right now we have to find her. She needs our help, and she doesn't even know it."

A lightbulb went off in Riley's head. "I know exactly where she's at! Let's go!"

CHAPTER 20

Search & Seizure

"Where are we going, Riley?" Robin asked. "I'm getting tired of driving, and I haven't seen my sister yet."

"Ladies, we're going where the trains roll," Riley said, leading them on an unexpected journey.

"What does that mean, 'where the trains roll'?"

"You'll find out soon enough. Make a right at this light and drive under the bridge. Then drive to the top of the hill. We'll have to walk the rest of the way." They were somewhere close to the port now and could feel the temperature change. As they were driving up the hill, they could see a bunch of abandoned trains. They looked ancient and probably hadn't been used since the 1950s.

"Wow, I would've never even known this place was here," Robin said, sounding surprised. "I don't see her, though."

"You wouldn't. Y'all just follow me. Shane and I used to come here a lot when we skipped school to clear our heads."

"And smoke some weed," Brandi interjected, rolling her eyes.

"Yeah, that too."

Day started to turn to night, and it was getting really cold outside. There was a cool breeze coming off the water that they weren't used to.

"Hey! I see somebody up there," Marisa said with confusion. The girls all started to run at the same time. "It's Shane. It's Shane!" She was lying on the ground. Her pockets were inside out and the contents of her purse were in a pile next to her.

"Shane! Shane!" Robin yelled, shaking her. Shane did not respond. "Call nine-one-one! Now!"

They were all crying and trying to make sense of what was going on. Marisa was on the phone with the 911 operator, attempting to explain their location. Riley grabbed the phone from Marisa and was able to give much better directions.

Robin held Shane in her arms. Fear ran through her body at the thought of losing her sister. She pushed those thoughts from her head and began to pray. "Dear Lord, touch my sister today. We need you." Just as she completed her prayer, Shane began to cough. She was confused and incoherent, but she was alive and breathing. "Oh, thank God," Robin sighed.

Robin called her parents and told them to get to the hospital as soon as possible. She rode in the ambulance with Shane. Shane had tears streaming down her face, but her eyes were still closed. "Robin, what happened to me?"

"We don't know exactly, but we're gonna figure this out. Mom and Dad are going to meet us at the hospital. Don't worry, we'll get through this."

"Sissy, I messed up. I'm sorry."

"It's okay, Shane. It's okay."

The girls were in the car. Even without a permit, Riley volunteered to drive. "I really hope she's gonna be okay. I feel like this is all my fault," Riley said.

"Who went through her stuff? Why was it all over the ground?" Marisa asked, sounding worried.

"Who knows?" Brandi said in deep thought. "Who knows?"

When they all pulled up to the hospital, Shane and Robin's parents were close behind. "What happened?" Mr. Foster shouted, running from the car.

"My baby! Where is my baby?" Shane's mother could be heard before they even saw her. When she came into view, her blue eyes looked red and puffy. She looked like she had been crying all the way to the hospital.

Shane was rushed into the emergency room. They had already started an IV in the ambulance to replenish the fluids she had lost. Her mother and father hurried to the stretcher to be by her side. "Baby, are you okay?" her mother asked through her tears.

"I'm okay, Mom. Daddy, I'm sorry. I'm so sorry," she said, crying equally as hard as her mother.

"Don't beat yourself up, baby. Just let the doctors help you. You hear me?" her father said with love in his eyes. "We'll be right here."

Shane was taken in to see the doctors while they all eagerly waited to hear the results of her examination. "What's taking so long?" Robin asked as she leaned against her father's shoulder.

"Be patient, baby," her father reassured her. "I'm glad they are taking their time with her. After what you girls told me, Shane put herself in a dangerous situation."

"Why didn't I do something when she came home high? I was in denial," Mrs. Foster cried.

"Mom, we all were," Robin said, moving next to her mom to give her a hug.

"I don't know what would have happened if you girls hadn't ..." Mrs. Foster's voice trailed off, and she began to sob.

Brandi and Marisa rushed over to her. She was like a second mother to both of them. "Don't even think like that, honey," Mr. Foster said, trying to console her.

Just then Dr. Nguyen came out of the examination room to tell them how Shane was progressing. "She's going to be just fine," he said. "She has something she wants to tell you, though," he directed this comment to the Fosters and allowed them to enter the room and speak with her.

When her parents walked in, Shane was crying. "I'm so sorry. I have to tell you guys how this all happened." Shane told them everything. She told them about her pressures at school, about taking the uppers, and about smoking weed. She told them about the blackouts.

"My baby ..." Her mother hugged her tightly. "I'm mad, Shane. But you know Mama has your back. We'll get you the help you need. You just rest and get strong."

Her father rubbed her head. She looked up at him with sorrowful eyes. He was a man of few words, but there was support in his stare. "You'll be okay, baby. From now on, no more secrets. I think there are a few more people who want to talk to you too."

They left the room and her friends and sister walked in. They all looked like they had been crying for days. "Ugh, y'all look a hot mess. What happened?" Shane asked, trying to lighten the mood. "Well, at least I got a smile," she added.

Riley grabbed her hand. "I'm so sorry, Shane."

"Girl, this wasn't your fault. It was mine. I started taking more pills, not to mention the weed. I smoked to counter the effects. The doctor said that if I hadn't stopped now, the blackouts could have been permanent. I think I blacked out by the water. I vaguely remember people standing over me. I wanted to scream but couldn't find my voice, and I blacked out again."

"Oh, Shane," Robin said. "Something awful could have happened to you."

"I know, but let me finish. I came to again and couldn't stand up. The doctor said I may have had a seizure. He won't know until he gets the tests back. I could see my stuff everywhere, but I couldn't move. I was so scared. I didn't know if I would ever see any of you again. The next thing I knew, you were all there. You were like angels ... my angels." They all cried and held hands.

"No matter what happens, we always have your back," Brandi said, kissing Shane's forehead.

Shane was released from the hospital and was back at school by Monday. Nobody at school knew what had happened. The girls were like family, so it stayed between them. Nobody else needed to know.

CHAPTER 21

Marisa

How crazy had life been recently? It seemed like eons had passed and she still hadn't talked to Matthew. Right after all the drama with Shane, they had been thrust into midterms. There hadn't been any time for a serious face-to-face. Now that midterms were over, there were no more distractions. She sent him a text saying, "U free 2nite," and they made a date.

It was Friday and school was going to be out for two weeks. The girls were invited to so many Christmas parties and New Year's parties that they had to be selective in choosing which ones to attend. They chose to skip the Friday party, so this was Marisa's chance to let Matt know how she felt.

"Hey," she said, jumping in the car.

Matthew was sending a text when she got in. He had a mischievous grin on his face.

"What's up? Where did you want to go?"

"Huh?" he responded, seeming very distracted.

"Matt, what are you doing? You aren't even listening to me." This wasn't how Marisa saw the evening going. She thought he would be just as excited to see her as she was to see him, but he hadn't even made eye contact yet.

Matthew sped away from her house and finally started talking. He seemed distant, but Marisa couldn't put her finger on what was going on. "So, what's been going on with you?" he asked. "We haven't really talked in a long time."

"I know. Life's just been so crazy, but I've wanted to talk to you."

"Really? I couldn't tell," he spat.

"Matt, is there something wrong? You seem upset."

"Nothing is wrong. This was just unexpected. I haven't heard from you. You barely talk to me at school," he said, sounding a bit wounded.

"A lot happened that I can't explain. Just know that life is about to be normal again. I talked to Brandi about what happened between us, and—"

He stopped her abruptly. "I can't do this. I'm tired of hearing about Brandi. I don't want to come in between the two of you. I'm tired of the drama. I started dating somebody, Mari."

"Oh ..." was all she could say. She wanted to let him know that she had feelings for him, and that Brandi had given them her blessing. She wanted to tell him that their feelings weren't wrong and that they could give this thing a try, but it was too late. He had already moved on. She felt a tear roll down her cheek, and she wiped it away. She didn't want him to know that she was crying. She just wanted to put as much distance between them as possible.

"This was a bad idea. I didn't know that you were seeing somebody, Matt. Just drop me back at my house."

Matt could tell that Mari was upset. His heart softened, and he pulled into a vacant parking lot. He turned to her. She looked more beautiful at that moment than he had ever seen her before. "Mari, are you crying?"

"No, Matt, I'm not crying. You're right ... there has been a lot of drama." She couldn't bring herself to make him choose, not after she had messed everything up. If Matt found someone that he liked, then she was willing to let him go. "I never knew high school would be so crazy." She smiled at him. "I've enjoyed spending time with you, but I want you to be able to give your relationship one hundred percent, and you can't do that with me hanging around."

"Hanging around?" He laughed. "Marisa Maldonado doesn't hang around; people hang around her."

She was blushing now. "Mattie, I've enjoyed the time we spent together this year."

"Me too, Mari. Thanks for being there for me. I'm sorry that I complicated things for you."

"Don't you dare apologize. It takes two." And with that, it was over. Matt dropped her back home. She watched him drive away, knowing that they had missed out on something really great. But the timing was all wrong. Everything was just wrong. "Good luck, mi amore," she said aloud, then went to her room to mourn the love that never was.

CHAPTER 22

Brandi

Christmas break was on and popping. Brandi had plans with her girls all week, so tonight was date night. Brendon was picking her up at seven, and it was six thirty. She stood in front of her full-length mirror and admired her reflection. Raven was in her room, watching her every move.

"Hey, squirt! What are you planning for tonight?"

"Mom's taking me to pick out some movies. We are going to have girls' night."

"Oh, that sounds fun. I should be back in time to join you. Rent *Dreamgirls* for us so we can get our sing on." They loved watching *Dreamgirls* together. It was their movie.

"Okay, sis! Hey, that's the doorbell. It's probably Brendon. I'll get it for you so you can make your entrance."

"You're a girl after my own heart. I'm raising you up right," Brandi said with a wink. She kissed Raven as she ran to get the door.

Brendon was standing by the door talking to her mom when she came down the stairs. "I'll have her home at a decent hour, Mrs. Haywood," she heard him saying.

When Brendon saw Brandi, his voice trailed off. She had on a black pencil skirt with a shiny black-and-white-striped shirt, tucked in and accented with a wide belt that she borrowed from her mom. Needless to say, Brandi looked gorgeous. None of this was lost on her mother. "Brandi, I was just telling Brendon that you need to be in by ten."

"I will, Mom. I promised Raven that we would watch *Dreamgirls* when I got home."

"Again?" her mother asked.

"Yes, again. Okay, handsome, let's hit the road," she said, turning to Brendon. When they arrived at his car, he opened the door for her and she slid into the passenger seat.

"Where to?" Before she could get more words out, he kissed her. They were still in her driveway. "Are you crazy? My mom will see you."

"I had to." Brendon backed the car out of the driveway. "You look amazing tonight."

"Well, thank you. You ain't so bad yourself. So, where are you taking me? I was thinking Houston's. What were you thinking?"

"I was thinking the Hilton and room service."

Brandi's blood ran cold. *This again ...* she thought. "Brendon, I'm not ready for that. I'm just not." And just like that, the night went sour. His demeanor changed; he changed.

"Well, I don't want to go to Houston's."

"Okay, Houston's is out. Cheddar's is okay with me. What do you think?"

"I think that my stomach is starting to ache. I guess I'm not hungry after all."

"Brendon, don't do this tonight," she pleaded. "Let's just go and have dinner." Brandi wanted to cry. She wanted to date Brendon, but he was pressuring her too much for sex. She had already made her decision. She didn't care if she would be alone. She didn't care if he broke up with her. She wasn't compromising herself for him.

"Nah, B. You want me to give you what you want, but you don't wanna give me what I want." Brandi was shocked. Not only was he putting pressure on her, but he was just downright rude!

"Take me home, Brendon."

Brendon abruptly stopped the car. "Get out!" he yelled at her.

"What?"

"You heard me, get out. Put those shoes to good use."

"I will not!" she yelled.

He revved the engine and drove recklessly through the neighborhood. He screeched to a halt and stopped at an intersection because another car was coming toward them. "Get out of my car," he said calmly, and this time she gladly got out. Brandi left the door open and walked away. "Close the door, Brandi!" he yelled out.

"Close your own door, loser! I never want to see your ugly face again. You are garbage!" She got on the phone with Shane. "Yo, I'm down the street from you. Can you get Robin to come and pick me up? It's freezing. ... Yeah, I'm okay. ... I'll explain later."

CHAPTER 23

Shane

As soon as Shane hung up the phone with Brandi, she ran to Robin's room. She saw her sister crying into her pillow. "Can't you knock first, Shane?"

"I'm sorry. It's Brandi. That creep Brendon left her on the side of the road. I don't know what happened, but she wants us to pick her up. Will you take me?"

"Of course," Robin said, drying her eyes.

When they got in the car, Shane turned to Robin. "Robie, what's wrong? Why were you crying?"

"I have something to tell you, Shane. I haven't wanted to worry you with my problems. I know it's been a stressful time for you."

"What, Robie? What is it?"

"I'm pregnant." Shane didn't know what to say. She just stared at her sister. She had been with her boyfriend for a little less than a year. How could this have happened? She knew that their lives were about to change. A tear rolled down her cheek.

"It's okay, Robin. I'll help you … whatever you need. I'll always be here for you."

Then Robin started to cry again. "Thanks, Shane," she sniffed.

They spotted Brandi and flashed the headlights. Shane rolled down the window, "Oh, you fancy, huh?" she asked, laughing a little at her friend's predicament.

"Oh, you funny, huh?" Brandi shot back at her. It was freezing outside, and Brandi was not dressed for the weather. "Thanks,

Robin," Brandi said, getting into the car and shivering the whole time.

"Girl, anytime. So what happened to you? How'd you wind up getting kicked to the curb?" Robin laughed. Brandi's drama was a nice break from her own.

"Robin, can you wait for me to thaw out before you start making jokes?" Brandi asked through chattering teeth. "That loser wanted to take me to the Hilton. He keeps trying to pressure me to have sex, but I'm not ready. I know that I'm not ready."

Robin pulled the car over again.

"Uh-oh ... last time that happened, I wound up walking. Why are you pulling over?"

"All jokes aside, girls, I don't want you to make the same mistakes that I've made. Don't have sex. The price is too great." Robin started to cry again.

"Don't worry about it, Robin. I told you that I told him no, I promise. I'm not having sex."

Shane rubbed her sister's back. She had never seen her cry so much. This explained why Robin was sleeping a lot and overeating. She had been going through all of this on her own and Shane never knew. She was so wrapped up in drugs that her sister had been on her own. Shane started to cry too.

"What's going on here? Why all the tears, Fosters?"

"I'm pregnant, Brandi."

"Oh, Robin ..." Robin was like a sister to Brandi. "I'm sorry, honey," Brandi said, teary-eyed. They knew that Robin had been destined for great things. This was going to seriously derail her plans. "Okay, on the bright side ... this baby is going to be super-duper fly. *And* you have the three best babysitters on this side of the Mississippi," she said with a country twang. Robin smiled. They hugged each other awkwardly in the car. Apparently drama was always just a day away.

Epilogue

$\mathcal{I}$t seemed like their break was flying by. Christmas had come and gone, and it was time to celebrate New Year's. It was the Fosters' tradition to throw a party for the girls at their home. This was going to be even more special because they were allowed to invite all of their friends.

The party was in full swing by ten. Everyone was there, including Brandi's and Marisa's parents. They stopped by to check on the girls and bring more food and drinks. Shane's mother directed them to the kitchen, where they set up homemade tamales, queso dip, fajitas, quiche, Buffalo wings, eggnog, and a large crystal bowl filled with a deliciously fruity punch.

Shane was talking to Riley, who had totally changed her lifestyle after what had happened. The Fosters had a long talk with Riley before she was allowed back into Shane's life. They knew that Shane was an independent girl, so they didn't blame Riley for what happened. They were concerned for both girls' well-being.

Brandi was chatting with Alex and some of the other cheerleaders. They were laughing as they reminisced about camp and football season. Raven had just arrived with Catherine, Brandi's mom, and was running around looking as cute as ever in her snow boots with pink fuzzy balls hanging on the sides. She ran over to Brandi and gave her a hug. "B, can I stay? Can I stay? Mom's about to go to church for the candlelight service, but I want to stay with you."

"We'll see, Raven. Go ask Mom first." And with that, Raven ran off excitedly.

"She's cute, Brandi. We need to make her a mini-uniform for basketball season. She can come on the court with us," Alex said.

"Girl, you don't know what you're in for. I'll see what my mom says. Raven would love that!"

Marisa and Hayley were hanging out close to the fireplace, drinking some eggnog. They were sad to see football season end. Twirling was now behind them, but they both played on the soccer team and looked forward to next semester.

Robin came halfway down the stairs and gestured for the girls to meet up in her room. One by one the three of them filed in and sat down on Robin's bed. "I have something for y'all," she said, pulling out beautifully wrapped platinum-colored boxes.

"What is this?" Marisa asked.

"Look, I know that you're just starting high school, and it can definitely be hard. You won't always be on a high school high. This is my last year, and I feel like I let the three of you down. Here is my way of saying that I'm sorry." By this time, Robin was crying. "I'm the only big sister y'all have."

"Girl, we can't take nine months of tears. You're gonna have to control yourself," Brandi joked.

"I know," she said, laughing. "Okay, I'm going to get through this. So, I was thinking, I don't want you to make the same mistake that I made. I had sex before I was ready, and I know that you're gonna be pressured by somebody to do it before you're ready too."

"You are preaching to the choir," Brandi chimed in.

"Well ... you're never really ready in high school ... no matter what anybody says. Okay, enough of the intro. Open your gifts."

They tore open the boxes and found beautiful rings inside. Each band was decorated with a rose, which held a small diamond in the center of the flower.

"The diamonds aren't big or anything, but they stand for purity. They stand alone, and they stand strong. This is my prayer for each of you. If you're ever put in a situation and you need the strength to stand, look down at your hand. You will all be in this fight together. Standing together."

"This is awesome. It's beautiful. Thank you, Robin." They were hugging Robin and thanking her all at the same time.

When they were walking down the stairs, Brandi said, "Wow, this is the first time that none of us have dates for New Year's Eve."

"Yep!" Mari said. "And I think I like it that way."

"Me too," Shane agreed. "I'm just happy we're all together. After all that we've been through with Ashley, Matthew, Brendon, ME ... this is the best way to bring in the New Year ... just us." She smiled.

"Stay right there," Shane's mother called out, watching them descend. She snapped their picture, capturing that moment forever.

Close to midnight, all the guests had their New Year's kit: whistles, hats, confetti, and champagne flutes filled with nonalcoholic punch or apple cider. The girls stood close to each other and chatted with their friends and family. "Three ... two ... one ... Happy New Year!"

As they lifted their glasses to toast the year to come, their diamond rings sparkled under the chandelier's light as a symbol of their purity and strength.

It was over. They had survived their first semester at Port City High. It wasn't easy, but they did it. It left each of them wondering what else high school had in store for them. What else?

ABOUT THE AUTHOR

Shannon Freeman

Born and raised in Port Arthur, Texas, Shannon Freeman works full time as an English teacher in her hometown. After completing college at Oral Roberts University, Freeman began her work in the classroom teaching English and oral communications. At that time, the characters of her breakout series, Port City High, began to form, but these characters would not come to life for years. An apartment fire destroyed almost all of the young teacher's worldly possessions before she could begin writing. With nothing to lose, Freeman packed up and headed to Los Angeles, California, to pursue a passion that burned within her since her youth, the entertainment industry.

Beginning in 2001, Freeman made numerous television appearances and enjoyed a rich life full of friends and hard work. In 2008, her world once again changed when she and her husband, Derrick Freeman, found out that they were expecting their first child. Freeman then made the difficult decision to return to Port Arthur and start the family that she had always wanted.

At that time, Freeman returned to the classroom, but entertaining others was still a desire that could not be quenched. Being in the classroom again inspired her to tell the story of Marisa, Shane, and Brandi that had been evolving for almost a decade. She began to write and the Port City High series was born.

Port City High is the culmination of Freeman's life experiences, including her travels across the United States and Europe. Her stories reflect the friendships she's made across the globe. Port City High is the next breakout series for today's young adult readers. Freeman says, "The topics are relevant and life changing. I just hope that people are touched by my characters' stories as much as I am."